# The Aussie Switch

## You Can't Tell The Players Without A Program

**By Jerry Bader**

MRPwebmedia.com/books
Amazon.com/author/jerrybader

# The Aussie Switch

## You Can't Tell The Players Without A Program

Written by Jerry Bader

Illustrations by Paola Ceccantoni


ISBN Paperback: 978-1-988647-56-2
Hard Cover: 978-1-988647-57-9
Ebook: 978-1-988647-58-6

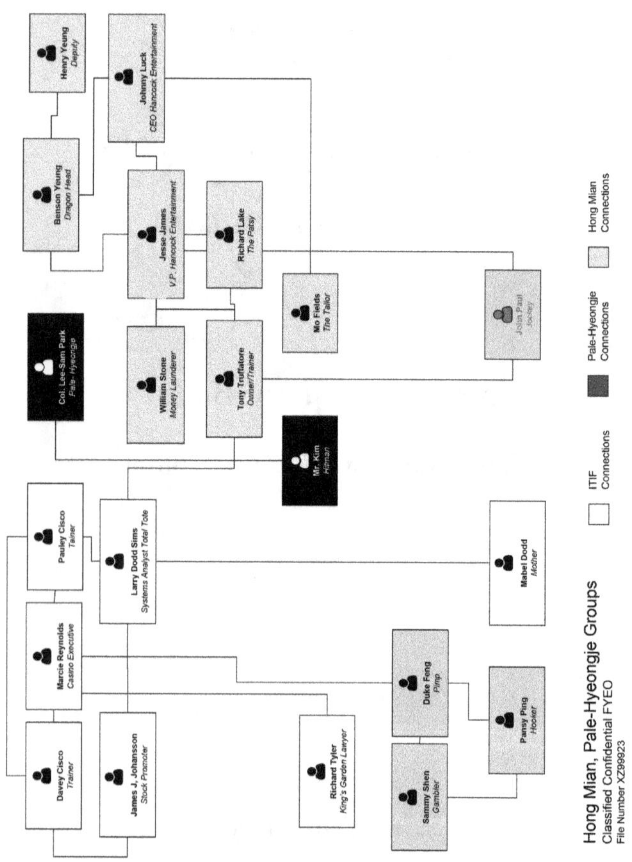


## HONG MIAN, PALE-HYEONGJE GROUPS
## CLASSIFIED CONFIDENTIAL FYEO

## A NEW DAY

## Part One

## 1
## A New Day

It all came to shit. Perhaps it's something in his DNA. No matter how hard he tried, everything ultimately went sideways. Australia, Los Angeles, it didn't seem to matter. The story was always the same.

Things started out great, then something went wrong, or someone got twitchy and made a mistake. It could have worked. It did work, at least for a while, but one bad break led to another, and then another, until you find yourself engulfed in the middle of a shit storm.

He started over before; he could start over again. Maybe this time, it will be different; maybe, the third time will be the charm. Tomorrow, he'd be on a new continent; two down, five more to go, well, four really, unless someone figures out how to race penguins. He smiled visualizing a row of flightless, tuxedo-clad birds all lined up in a mini starting gate itching to waddle their way to the finish line.

He fumbled for the light switch. 'Christ he could have left a light on. What the hell was he thinking: saving money for the motel owner, typical.'

Finally, he finds the switch and flicks it on. The staccato blinking of cheap florescent lights blinds him for a moment. As his eyes become accustomed to the stark, harsh lighting, he sees his brother head down on the desk taking a nap. 'Christ, how could he sleep at a time like this?'

He scans the room: your standard second-rate motel. His brother's suitcase is sitting on the bed. He opens it. Both their passports lay open on top of the neatly packed clothes.

His brother must have taken a sleeping pill or something to calm his nerves. It obviously did the trick. He is out to the world. He walks over and shakes him. No response. He shakes him harder, again no response. Something is wrong. He lifts his brother's head… "Goddamn it!"

A small round hole in the middle of his forehead stares back at him as if to say, 'you really screwed the pooch this time brother.' No blood, no exit wound, just a hole in his forehead, and dead eyes.

He knows what caused it. Bastards! They couldn't just shoot him like normal murderers; they had to use a bolt pistol like he was some lame, used-up crowbait ready for the Mexican meat market.

He stands there a minute just staring. It's like looking in a mirror. The face with the newly added cavity could be his. If he'd been in the room instead of his brother, it would have. Twins are supposed to have a special affinity; if one twin stubs his toe, the other feels the pain, but that must be a myth because he never felt that kind of connection. Still, they were always there for one another, no matter what kind of trouble they got in, and there was always trouble. It's the business; nobody gets away clean, that's not the way the game is played. Everyone is a cheat, it's just a matter of degree; some are just bigger crooks than others.

Nostalgia isn't helpful, not for him or for his brother, besides he had a plane to catch: a new continent, a new city, a fresh start. He takes out his cell phone and sends a text to Marcie. He goes to the bed, picks up both passports and puts one in each pocket of his camel cashmere sport coat. You never know when an extra identity might come in handy. Tomorrow would be a new day.

**THE CISCO BROTHERS**

# 2
# The Cisco Brothers

**Six Months Earlier...**

Davey and Pauley Cisco, the Cisco twins, are Australian horse trainers. Like other identical twins, they look, dress, and act as if they were a single entry. At thirty-six they still managed to be equal in just about every physical manifestation you can imagine. Age had not yet diminished their indistinguishable good looks or athletic bodies, even the white forelock that magically appeared on both men over the last year matched.

People had trouble telling the two men apart, a fact that in their early days worked to their financial advantage, but that deception stopped when Davey kept getting suspended for multiple infractions ranging from illegal performance enhancing drugs to falsified clocking times. All trainers do it, it's a fact of horse racing life, but the smart ones keep the suspensions to a minimum.

If the two men differ in any substantial way, it is their approach to life; Davey is reckless, outspoken, and willing to risk everything on a horse, a scheme, or a dame. The bigger the odds, the more Davey is prepared to go all in, a fact that didn't go down well with his wife, Marcie, who finally had enough. She divorced Davey to concentrate on her job as an executive in a Macau casino.

Pauley on the other hand is more circumspect, more calculating, and far more careful. Eventually Pauley also got fed-up being mistaken for his more flamboyant, rule bending brother, and decided to take his skills to sunny Southern California where he could re-establish his reputation at the Hancock Racetrack.

It was only a matter of time before Davey showed up at Pauley's Hancock Arms front door; the Aussie racing muck-a-mucks suggested in the most forceful manner that perhaps it would be better if Davey pursued his career as far away from the New South Wales racing fraternity as possible.

And so Davey and Pauley both became successful California-based thoroughbred horse trainers. Both enjoyed success and the good life, but each in his own way: Pauley pursuing a judicious calculated approach, while Davey plunged headlong into a more aggressive pursuit of life, love, and the big score.

**THE TICKET SCAM**

# 3
# The Ticket Scam

Richard Lake is new to the Hancock surveillance team. He is assigned to the race-track investigation unit watching pari-mutuel agents and bettors, looking for anything out of the ordinary, anything that will alert his bosses to a scam. The Shanghai Players' Club is located adjacent to the track. It's where Jesse James, Vice President of Operations has her office. Lake manages to convince Jesse's secretary that he has something important to show her. He's ushered into Jesse's private office.

Jesse: "Richard... isn't it?

Lake: "Yes Ma'am, Richard Lake, you hired me to work on the surveillance unit."

Jesse smiles: "I'm not your mother or the Queen, so you can call me Jesse. What I call you depends on what you tell me."

Lake hands Jesse a disc. "Take a look. See for yourself. You tell me if I'm wasting your time."

Jesse puts the disc into her computer. A video starts running automatically with a date and time stamp across the bottom. A man in a Yankee baseball cap approaches one of the self-service betting machines. He swipes his account card and punches in his PIN number. He takes a stack of tickets wrapped in a thick rubber band out of his pocket. He sticks the tickets one at a time into the machine. Jesse looks at Lake.

Lake: "Keep watching." The man proceeds to cash fifteen tickets one by one. "That's a lot of tickets. It got me curious, so I kept an eye on this guy." The video ends and another starts. The same day, fifteen minutes later. The same guy approaches another machine and cashes another ten or fifteen winning tickets.

Lake: "Something is definitely fishy, so I check out the accounts. The first set of tickets worth seven-thousand-dollars went into an account for a Mabel Dodd, and the second set of tickets for twelve thousand went into an account for a Marcie Reynolds. I think it's safe to assume the person in the video isn't Mabel Dodd or Marcie Reynolds."

Jesse: "He's a trainer, one of the Cisco twins. I can't tell which one, but if there's something shady going on, it's probably Davey."

Lake: "Keep watching, there's more."

Another video starts. It's time stamped an hour before the previous videos. This time Cisco is sitting in the Hancock snack bar nursing a cup of coffee.

Lake: "Watch carefully." As Cisco takes a sip of coffee someone in a matching Yankee baseball cap pulled down covering most of his face walks by and casually places a folded newspaper on the table occupied by Cisco. He doesn't stop; he keeps on walking. Cisco reaches into the folded newspaper and carefully removes two stacks of tickets wrapped in thick elastic bands.

Jesse: "Who's the second Yankee fan."

Lake: "I checked all the footage. There wasn't one good image of his face. He must know where all the cameras are. The thing is, this isn't an isolated incident. This series of events happens once a week.

Jesse: "But all the tickets are legit?"

Lake: "Yeah... they're all legit, but they're all old uncashed tickets about to expire."

Jesse: "Something is going on. I want you to keep an eye on these guys. I'm transferring you to the Shanghai surveillance unit. I'll have the techs set you up so you have access to the club and the track."

Lake: "Why the club?"

Jesse: "Davey Cisco has a weekly poker game in one of the Club's private rooms. Maybe there's a connection. Maybe one of his poker buddies is the other Yankee fan."

Lake: "It's possible Cisco and his poker pals have some kind of legitimate betting pool."

Jesse: "Sure... and if pigs had wings, they'd still wallow in the mud. Davey Cisco is a shyster."

**THE GEEK**

# 4
## The Geek

Larry Dodd Sims is your classic geek, a twenty-nine-year-old man-boy obsessed with competitive gaming, also known as e-sports. To be clear, Larry is no nerd, no Coke bottle glasses, pocket-protector, socially awkward misfit; no, Larry is your average, nondescript, fade into the woodwork, computer programmer with an IQ of one-hundred-and-forty. Larry graduated from MIT with an advanced computer degree, but rather than getting a job like normal people, he decided he'd rather play. His first love was online poker resulting in a nice little nest egg of four-hundred-and-fifty-thousand dollars.

With success comes arrogance, and a perspective that failure is for other, less intelligent people, not for Larry Dodd Sims. So Larry decided to take on the world of live tournament poker where he had to sit in an overcrowded room that reeked of nervous energy and sweat. His mother, Mabel, warned him that dealing with people was not his forte, and that he should stick to computers. Perhaps a nine-to-five job would be an appropriate option, but Larry was determined to give tournament poker a try. As it turned out, sitting at a table with five real people whose approach to the game of poker relied as much on psychology as card counting and odds' calculating was a mistake. Larry proceeded to lose almost all of his online winnings.

His widowed mother was displeased. She relied on her only son to pay the rent and keep her in booze and bingo money. Without a steady flow of cash, how could she survive? He owed her, and she demanded he live up to his responsibilities. To appease her disappointment, Larry got a job, as Chief Systems Analyst at Total Tote System Incorporated, the leading pari-mutuel operator in the USA with a seventy-five percent market share. The company has installations in the majority of racetracks and off track betting establishments in the country, including the Hancock Racetrack run by Jesse James. But having a regular job still left plenty of time for Larry to pursue his more satisfying gaming interests.

So Larry found an obscure, somewhat bizarre South Korean game called *Dunoe Segseu*, in English, Brain Sex, or what its fanatical adherents call Brain Fucking; nobody said it makes sense, it's grown men sitting in front of computers trying to outwit international players in a psychological game of hide and seek. Each gamer pays a minimum entrance fee of fifty US dollars in order to play. The big games, or the *Keun Sigan*, require a thousand-dollar ante. The player is then given a random psychological profile that could be anything ranging from a serial killer to an accountant, and a goal that requires the winner to outsmart all the other players in the game.

*Dunoe Segseu* is a twenty-four/seven addiction; new games are started once a pot reaches a designated pot size. Larry only plays *Keun Sigan*; why waste time on the small stuff?

Larry, like most of the game's enthusiasts is a fanatic, and many are more than a bit crazy. The company, SKE-Sport, takes fifty percent of the entrance fee off the top, and the winner of each game is credited with the rest. If there's no winner SKE takes the pot. Within six months, Larry Dodd Sims, known to his South Korean fans as the *Jeonja Kauboi*, the Electronic Cowboy, amassed a tidy one-hundred-and-sixty-three million South Korean Won stake, or a little over one-hundred-and-fifty-thousand US dollars, all of it sitting in a downtown Seoul bank account.

As the *Jeonja Kauboi*, Larry was a South Korean e-sport god, but before he was able to reach his Electronic Cowboy status, he was a consistent loser. Larry used his computer savvy skills to hack the SKE-Sport servers and what he found was to say the least interesting. The game was fixed, not surprising, considering what he found after some further research. Following the trail of numbered companies led to an Isle of Man corporation owned by seven South Korean ex-military officers known as the *Pal-e Hyeongje*, Brothers In Arms, the most dangerous criminal organization in South Korea with tentacles in every Korean community across the United States. The skill needed to beat the most dangerous criminal enterprise in South Korea was definitely a source of satisfaction, but winning the actual games was rather hollow. The sport was in beating the system not playing the game; nevertheless, he continued to play, and work in order to satisfy his mother's ever-increasing financial demands. But his live tournament poker experience continued to eat-away at him.

Larry Dodd Sims has to win at everything he does. It's an obsession. If he can't win by skill or intellect, he'll cheat, but win he will, no matter the stakes or the consequences.

He could always make money that wasn't the issue; it was winning that counted. His tournament poker failure would not be allowed to stand. It was time to give the game another try. He decided backroom private cash games were more to his enochlophobia liking, rather than the over-crowded, concentration-distracting Casino sponsored marathons.

It is at just such a private room at the Shanghai Players' Club that Larry Dodd Sims met Davey Cisco, kindred spirits, each with a fixation for winning, no matter how high the cost.

The Shanghai Players' Club is part of the elaborate Hancock Complex, an ever-expanding real estate, entertainment, and gambling district that includes a hotel, condos, a racetrack, casino, the

Shanghai Players' Club, and a variety of bars, restaurants, and theatres. It's Disneyland for people with too much money.

The complex is owned by a syndicate of organizations that treat legalities as minor inconveniences. Problems are solved by employing financial influence, or if necessary, more extreme methods of persuasion. The complex is run by a handsome Chinese-American version of Jay Gatsby, with the able assistance of his beautiful blonde protégé, an ex-jockey, and all-around female badass, Jesse James.

Every week Jesse arranges for Davey and friends to meet in a private room at the Shanghai Players Club. The club supplies an attractive cheongsam dressed dealer and an equally comely hostess that serves drinks, food, and visual distraction. The minimum initial buy-in is ten-thousand-dollars, and the house takes a ten percent cut off-the-top of every pot.

The four mainstays of the poker group are Davey Cisco, fellow owner-trainer Tony Truffatore, computer wizard and gambler, Larry Dodd Sims, and boiler-room stock promoter, James J. Johansson. Davey's brother Pauley makes an occasional appearance plus a rotating group of wealthy businessmen who get their kicks out of slumming with the colorful horse racing insiders.

**THE POKER GAME**

# 5
## The Poker Game

Tonight the private lounge in the Shanghai Players' Club is occupied by the usual Thursday night suspects: Davey Cisco, Larry Dodd Sims, Jimmy Johansson, and Tony Truffatore.

Buffalo native, Tony Truffatore is one of the best trainers in the country, but his past checkered personal life often got him into trouble. Trouble that led to associations with people like Hancock CEO and triad big shot, Johnny Luck, *enfant terrible*, Jesse James, and upstate New York mobster, Nicky, The Mushroom, Fungo.

Tony is currently enjoying a run of good luck, a pleasant change from his previous difficulties. He inherited a large stable of high-priced racehorses from the estate of his ex-employer, Mrs. Josephine Somersby Murphy, who died in a questionable car accident in Palermo, Sicily. As the new owner of Peanut Spread Stables, Tony figured he'd be welcomed into the fraternity of fat-cat thoroughbred racehorse owners, but entrée into horse racing's upper crust took more than ownership. Even the late unlamented Mrs. Murphy was not a bona fide society type. Her money came from her husband's seemingly legal commercial endeavors, a fact that could be disputed if you knew the actual details. Murphy's brother, Governor Samuel Somersby, is a high profile politician, a slimy enough vocation that might be tolerated at fund-raisers and dinners, but otherwise, a significant class demerit point.

Tony couldn't even rise to Murphy's hold-your-nose status. He is just another working stiff who happens to own horses. If you couldn't trace your heritage back to some pre Civil War slave owner, you were just another *nouveau riche* wannabe. In Tony's case, his Calabrese grandfather's Porcini farmer occupation precluded him of ever making it onto horse racing's social register. And so Tony ignored the society slight, and instead, found solace in the company of more colorful men, men who found most of society's rules mere optional suggestions.

One of these men is Jimmy Johansson. James J. Johansson is a shark, a *gonef* in a five-thousand-dollar custom-made Mo Field's suit. Let there be no misunderstanding, Jimmy Johansson is a crook. When asked by newspaper reporters about his frequent stock market scandals, Jimmy always pleaded his innocence. He characterized himself as a victim whose good nature and faith in his fellow man caused him no-end of personal distress. He always showed sympathy for those investors that met their financial undoing. The fact that Jimmy's own bank balance continued to swell to the point of embarrassment is evidence that he, like others in the stock manipulation business, live in a post truth world where alternative facts stand-in for reality. Jimmy's knack of avoiding lengthy prison terms is the result of his unique ability to always find a patsy: a sacrificial lamb the authorities could lead to the virtual execution-alter.

Tonight's poker game is two hours old and Tony is the big loser; he's down fifteen-thousand-dollars. He's already bought-in for a second ten thousand and a half of that is gone. He's considering buying-in for another five. Each man tosses two one-hundred-dollar chips into the middle of the table. Lana, the dealer, gathers the chips into a single pile. She distributes two cards face down to each player as Rachel, the hostess, distributes fresh Rye and Gingers to each man.

Johansson lifts the corners of his cards revealing a Three of Hearts and an Ace of Spades; Tony slides his cards towards his body and carefully sneaks a peek keeping both cards close to his body. He's got a Five of Diamonds and an Ace of Diamonds. Davey picks up his cards not concerned that someone might steal a look. He has a Jack of Hearts and an Ace of Clubs. Larry doesn't bother to look. He just leaves his cards face down on the table. He pushes five-hundred-dollars worth of chips into the middle of the table. Each man follows matching Larry's bet.

Lana buries a card and places three new cards face-up in the middle of the green felt, a Three of Spades, a Five of Clubs, and a Jack of Diamonds. Johansson has a pair of Threes, Tony a pair of

Fives, and Davey a pair of Jacks. Sims' cards are still faced-down on the table. He hasn't bothered to look at them, a fact that could be construed as arrogance or stupidity. Poker is as much a game of psychology as it is cards, and so Larry's strategy is an attempt to psych out his opponents.

Sims shuffles a stack of chips in one hand like a practiced magician. He adds a thousand dollars to the pot. Johansson follows quickly matching Sims' raise. Davey looks at each man trying to catch a tell but none is visible. He adds his thousand to the pile. Tony hesitates. He's already down fifteen-thousand-dollars; this is becoming an expensive evening. If he loses much more, he may have to sell Gonzo Ralph, a promising two-year-old chestnut.  He takes the plunge and adds his chips.

Lana buries a card and adds the Turn to the three already on the table. It's a Four of Diamonds. Nothing has changed. Sims checks. Davey is sitting with a pair of Jacks with no other picture cards in the flop. He's covered if an Ace comes up unless someone is already sitting with two in their hand. Checking is the safe bet, he can always raise on the River.

Everyone checks. They're all playing the waiting game; no one wants to show their strength or weakness. Lana buries another card and adds the River to the flop. It's a Two of Clubs. The room is silent. Rachel breaks the spell by dropping an ice cube into a glass. The sound of Ginger Ale commingling with Rye over the crackling cold ice cubes sounds like the thunder of Niagara Falls.

Larry Dodd Sims pushes all his chips into the center of the table. "All-in!" He still hasn't looked at his cards.

Tony looks at Larry like he's crazy. "Jesus Christ, Larry, you don't even know what you got." Larry just sits back in his chair and takes a sip of Rye and Ginger.

Davey smiles in admiration of his gambling friend. "You really are one fucking crazy son-of-a-bitch."

Johansson stares at his chips for what seems like a very long time. Tony is nervous. He can't cover the bet. It will cost him everything he's got left and more. "It's your play Jimmy," says Truffatore, "what's it going to be? You in or out?" Johansson matches Sims' bet.

"Fuck it!" Davey pushes all his chips into the pile. "It's up to you Tony. You going to play with the big boys or are you going to wimp-out on us?"

Tony looks at his cards again, a pair of fives, no wait; he's got a Five-high straight. Shit! Tony pushes in all his chips. "And I'll raise. I'll put up Gonzo Ralph; he's worth at least fifty-thousand-dollars."

The men all look at Davey to confirm Truffatore's claim. "Yeah, the horse is worth at least that much, but I think you're buffing. I'm in. Johansson and Sims each match Truffatore's bet.

"Read'em and weep boys." Tony doesn't wait his turn he just flips over his cards, "Five-high straight."

Davey laughs and turns over his cards, "Five-high straight. Guess I got half of your horse, my friend."

"Not so fast fellows," says Johansson, "you better cut that chestnut into threes." He reveals his matching Five-High straight. They all look at Sims. He shrugs and flips over one of his cards; it's a Nine of Spades. Nothing. He flips over the second card; it's an Ace of Hearts.

"No fucking way!" blurts Tony, "five matching straights. That just can't happen!"

Davey: "While it appears it just did."

Sims: "How we going to divvy up the horse?"

Johansson: "I've got an idea." Lana and Rachel take the house's final cut and leave, each pocketing a healthy tip. The four men are left with drinks, a pile of chips, an IOU for Gonzo Ralph, and a problem of how to split the horse.

## THE ROOM

# 6
# The Room

The sign on the door to the floor above the Shanghai Players' Club is marked "Storage, Employees Only." In fact, the entire floor is a surveillance operation that houses sophisticated video and audio recording devices strategically hidden within the Chinese-inspired Art Déco interior furnishings of the club and its high stakes private rooms.

As is her custom, Jesse James makes her nightly appearance in the room, checking to see that everyone is awake and on the lookout for any shenanigans that might be taking place. You would think rich people wouldn't try to pull any shady shit, but you'd be wrong. Nobody likes to lose money, especially folks used to getting their own way.

You would think smart people would stay away from a place that is in the business of taking your money, but they don't. Rich or poor, smart or dumb, people are drawn to gambling like moths to a flame, and ultimately, they all get burnt. It turns out, rich people are as greedy, stupid, and vengeful as everybody else.

Richard Lake is the new guy on the Shanghai surveillance team, placed there to keep a close eye on Davey Cisco, suspected of being involved in some kind of crooked betting scheme. Lake spots Jesse making her rounds and waves to her to come over. Jesse approaches and leans over his shoulder, "What's up?"

Lake: "What are the odds of four guys coming up with matching straights?"

Jesse: "Are they playing Texas Hold'em?"

Lake: "Yeah"

Jesse: "Which dealer team?"

Lake: "Lana and Rachel."

Jesse: "We get our cut?"

Lake: "Sure, Lana even made sure we got our piece on a horse Truffatore put up."

Jesse: "So what's the problem?"

Lake: "I don't know. Davey Cisco is one of the players, but they're all kind of iffy. That Johansson is a real creep, maybe he's our Yankee fan. They're discussing how to split the pot and what to do with the horse."

Jesse: "Which horse is it?"

Lake: "Gonzo Ralph... take a listen." Lake hands Jesse the headphones. Jesse puts them on and points to a chair. Lake gets up and retrieves the chair. Jesse sits and listens. Lake finds another pair of headphones and plugs-in so he can hear what's being said…

Tony: "So I'll take my horse as part of my share of the pot."

Johansson: "What if we don't split the pot?"

Tony: "I'm not taking a chance on a winner-take-all!"

Sims: "You already did."

Tony: "I ducked a bullet once tonight, I'm not trying my luck again."

Johansson: "Nobody's talking about that. What if we roll the dough and Gonzo Ralph into a syndicate? Davey and I have been thinking about this for a while, The Thoroughbred Investment Fund?"

Davey: "How about The International Thoroughbred Investment Fund? We get some of those Arab *bizzillonaires* to cough-up some of their oil dough."

Tony: "Who's going to invest in an unproven horse?"

Davey: "Horses... we use the money Jimmy raises to buy more horses. It's the potential we'd be selling. There are always suckers looking for the next fucking Native Dancer. You know how many guys wouldn't think twice about dropping a few grand just to say they got a piece of a potential Derby winner. They can't buy the Dodgers, but maybe they can own a piece of the next American Pharoah. Who the hell wouldn't want a piece of that? I love it. I'll get Pauley to come in with us. A little extra starting capital won't hurt."

Tony: "So how do we make money out of this?"

Davey: "Jesus Tony, you're no virgin. We charge the Fund for everything, commissions on the purchase of the horses, training, racing, every-thing, and of course we draw salaries for being on the board."

Johansson: "What if we build-in a betting com-ponent?"

Tony: "What do you mean?"

Johansson: "Owners are going to want to bet on the horses, so we do it for them."

Davey: "How would that work?"

Sims: "That's where I come in. I can analyze the odds and place the bets based on a Multinomial Logit Regression."

Tony: "A what?"

Sims: "Don't worry about it. I know what I'm doing."

Tony: "I don't get it."

Sims: "I have access to all the statistical information we need.  We do it right, we should get a twenty to twenty-five percent return on the money; worst case scenario we get fifteen to nineteen percent ROI."

Tony: "Yeah but it's racing, anything can happen. You guys know there's no guarantee, even when the fix is in. There's just too many variables, we lose the investors dough and they'll scream bloody murder."

Sims: "So what? Let them scream. Horse racing is a gamble, sometimes you win and sometimes you lose, besides all we need to do is turn Gonzo Ralph into the second coming of Secretariat. Nobody will want to jump ship before the stud fees start pouring in. As long as Gonzo Ralph has a shot at the big three, people will be happy sitting back sucking down Mint Juleps in the owner's box."

Tony: "And if someone wants out, and we don't have the cash?"

Johansson: "We pay them out from new investment."

Tony: "That a Ponzi scheme. What if we get caught?"

Johansson: "Have faith my friend. I've pulled off this kind of thing before. What we need is a patsy, someone we can nominally put in charge. If things go sideways, he's the one that goes down, not us. We're just innocent investors who trusted the wrong fellow."

Jesse takes off her headphones while still staring at the computer monitor.

Lake: "Did you hear those guys?"

Jesse looks over at Lake. "You got a nice suit?"

Lake: "Nah... what do I need a suit for?"

Jesse takes a business card out of her pocket and hands it to him. He looks at it and then at Jesse. "Three Kings... I can't afford a Mo Fields' suit."

Jesse: "Just tell Mo to charge my office." She looks at his Adidas and Old Navy jeans. "You'll also need some custom shirts, ties, and some new shoes. Mo will set you up."

Lake: "What do I need all that for?"

Jesse: "You are The International Thoroughbred Investment Fund's new patsy.

Lake: "Me?"

Jesse: "Think of it as a promotion." She gets up and starts to walk away.

Lake calls after her: "But I don't know what to do?"

Jesse turns, "Exactly… that makes you perfect for the job. From now on you report only to me. I'll call Mo in the morning and tell him to expect you, then come see me for instructions."

**THE PATSY**

# 7
## The Patsy

Tony Truffatore sits in the reception area of the Shanghai Players' Club. When he arrived home after his weekly poker game, there was a message waiting for him on his home phone, "Get your ass to my office eleven o'clock tomorrow morning. And keep your mouth shut - JJ" Jesse was her usual charming self.

Truffatore had no idea why he was being summoned, but if Jesse called, you best answer, or your next visit might be from Mo Fields, and he wouldn't be measuring you for a new suit. To the general public, Mo Fields is the top tailor in Los Angeles with A-List clients his competitors would die for; but Fields had a second profession as a contract killer for the Hong Mian. The same triad organization that employs Jesse and Johnny Luck. Jesse and Mo may not be Chinese, but when they come calling, you better snap to attention because whatever they say comes directly from Dragon Head Benson Yeung or his righthand man, Johnny Luck.

Jesse enters the office trailed by a young man who looks like a reject from Silicon Valley. She says good morning to the receptionist and enters the private office area. She waves to Tony to follow her. Jesse greets her secretary, enters her office, and flops down in a large brown leather office chair behind an enormous Bauhaus desk that dwarfs her ex jockey-sized body. She points to the two chairs facing her desk. Tony takes one while Richard Lake takes the other. The receptionist enters with a carafe of fresh coffee and buttered raisin toast. She pours three cups, handing one to Tony, one to Lake, and one to Jesse.

Jesse: "You guys want some toast?" Tony shakes his head, but Lake takes a piece. Jesse sips her coffee. "Got to have a good breakfast Tony, it gets the metabolism started."

Truffatore: "You called, I'm here. What do you want?"

Jesse: "Jesus Tony... Is that any way to talk to an old pal? I'm doing you a favor?"

Truffatore: "Cut the shit Jesse, what do you want and how's it going to fuck me?"

Jesse takes a bite of toast and another swig of hot coffee. She pauses for dramatic effect as she savors the toast and fresh brewed pick-me-up. "Tony... I'd like you to meet Richard Lake, your ITIF patsy."

Truffatore: "My what?"

Jesse: "I understand, you and your fellow poker miscreants are in need of a patsy for your cockamamie investment scam, and Richard here has kindly volunteered to provide his services."

Truffatore: "Come on Jesse, this has nothing to do with you and Johnny."

Jesse: "*Au contraire* my friend. You know better than to fuck with my racetracks."

Truffatore: "I wouldn't let him screw with any of your tracks here or up North."

Jesse: "Jesus… are you stupid. You think your playmates care if you end up in jail, or buried under a pile of horse shit? I'm doing you a solid. Take some advice. There are two kinds of people in the world, the Fuckers and the Fuckees. So which one are you?"

Truffatore looks at Lake: "How am I suppose to sell this kid to Johansson and Sims. He looks like he should be parking cars, not running an investment firm."

Jesse: "Don't you worry about that. He'll have all the right credentials and Mo is getting him all decked out in some nice new threads. You tell your partners that you found the perfect patsy, and you're bringing him to your next poker game."

Truffatore: "I don't know Jesse, what if they don't think he's right for the job?"

Jesse: "You make sure that doesn't happen."

Truffatore resigns himself to the inevitable. He stands up, grabs a piece of toast from Jesse's plate, and takes a big bite. "Just make sure the kid is ready for next Thursday, I'll tell the boys I found someone. Can I go now?"

Jesse: "Just one more thing. Why the hell would you bet Gonzo Ralph? He's got real potential."

Truffatore: "What can I say, I'm stupid."

Jesse smiles. She looks at Lake, "Hear that Richard, self-awareness is the first sign of enlightenment."

She looks at Tony, "I'm proud of you Tony, take another piece of toast."

Truffatore: "Fuck you Jesse." And he leaves.

## THE ITIF

## Part Two

## 8
## The ITIF

Over the next six months, the International Thoroughbred Investment Fund takes shape with Richard Lake as its CEO and public face. With the help of Jesse, Mo Fields, and Tony Truffatore, Richard Lake is turned into a distant American relative of Federico Tesio, the most famous breeder of racehorses in Italy, and probably the world. Tesio was responsible for breeding such legendary horses as Nearco, Ribot, Braque, and Cavaliere d'Arpino.

Tesio also wrote the definitive book on racehorse breeding entitled, *Puro-Sangue–Animale de Esperimento*, that Lake read in English, practically memorizing the entire volume. Richard's eidetic mind absorbed the fundamentals of breeding and the Tesio method as if he had been borne into it.

As President and CEO of ITIF, Lake spends his time glad-handing investors and being interviewed by the press. The female reporters are especially impressed by his charming manner, movie star good looks, and Mo Fields' wardrobe. Lake surprised himself at how easy it is to con potential marks with bullshit stories of visits to the Italian countryside where supposedly, he learned the intricacies of breeding champions from the granddaughter of the nephew of the great man himself. Whether Tesio, actually had a granddaughter, or a nephew made no difference, investors fell for the twaddle like lambs being led to the slaughter. Lake would setup the investor with his tales of secret breeding expertise, then Johansson would move in for the close.

If the vision of millions generated by the potential Gonzo Ralph stud fees, the leading two-year-old money-winner, didn't close the deal, then Johansson would pull the mark aside and explain the finer points of Multinomial Logit Regression. The complexities of which were explained to him by Sims, their covert computer savant, an insider with special access to information no one else is privy to. As an experienced conman, Johansson knew the best way to con a mark is to make them think they've got an illegal advantage; it's usually enough to close the deal with the added benefit of compromising the sucker with knowledge of their participation in an unlawful enterprise.

Tony Truffatore and Davey Cisco are in charge of new acquisitions while Larry Dodd Sims sets-up the computer-aided-betting system based on data he's gleamed from his day job as Chief Systems Analyst at Total Tote System Incorporated. The company gets off to a good start with Gonzo Ralph the shiny bauble dangled in front of investors, but once payouts become due, money gets tight. A financial crisis looms.

Richard Lake meets with Jesse at a suburban Dave and Busters every Friday to report the details of ITIF's operation. On this particular Friday Tony Truffatore is told to be at the meeting.

Tony enters Dave and Busters. He looks around, trying to spot Jesse. The place is crawling with teenagers and the noise is near deafening. He finally spots Jessie and Lake at some digital race-car arcade game. He approaches. "You kids having fun?"

Jesse and Lake continue to finish their game while Truffatore waits impatiently. They finally finish with Jesse winning.

Jesse: "Let's go to the restaurant where we can talk."

Tony: "Why are we meeting here?"

Jesse: "You'd rather meet at the ITIF offices? Use your head, your playmates aren't likely to be hanging out in a place like this, are they?"

Tony: "Makes sense I guess. So why do you want to meet with me, hasn't Lake filled you in?"

They get to the restaurant and take a booth. The waitress comes by and they order sandwiches and coffee. Lake looks at Tony: "You and Cisco have spent a lot of money on yearlings, and that doesn't bring in any cash. Sims' betting scheme is just breaking even; so much for artificial intelligence. After you deduct the money, you guys are taking out of the company, there's not a lot of working capital left. Gonzo Ralph has some nice earnings but not enough to sustain the operation. Investors are getting antsy. We're getting inquiries from some investors about pulling out. Johansson has been stalling them. He's trying to raise more capital to pay them out, but that well has run dry. It's only a matter of time before it all falls apart."

Tony: "We could sell the yearlings but we'd be lucky to breakeven. Gonzo Ralph might be the only option, but I won't be happy if we lose him."

Lake: "Johansson and Cisco won't go along with that either. I overheard them talking to Sims about some big computer score they got planned, a guaranteed Pick Six deal."

Tony: "The bastards didn't say a word to me. They must be planning to make one big score for themselves and leave you and I hung-out to dry."

Jesse: "Did you hear anything else?"

Lake: "The only other thing I heard is, it's planned for the next time Gonzo Ralph runs, the Mogul Invitational."

Jesse: "Any idea how they're going to pull it off?"

Tony: "Sims keeps bragging how he's been hacking some Korean e-game outfit for months. Says he's got a million dollars stashed away in a bank in Seoul. The guy is a computer genius, but crooked as a dog's hind leg. His plan has got to have something to do with Total Totes' computer system. Sims is their Chief Systems Analyst, so he has access to everything they got."

Jesse: "They probably have a way of fixing the winning tickets on some races. Gonzo Ralph will be a prohibitive favorite in the Mogul, so they don't have to worry about that race. That's how we'll fuck them."

Lake: "I don't get it."

Tony: "She means a ringer... we replace Gonzo Ralph with a look-alike that can't run. Then we bet on all the other horses in the race, hoping we catch a break and a long shot wins. We get a big payday and our partners get screwed."

Jesse: "Like I said Tony, you're either the Fucker or the Fuckee, but we need a Gonzo duplicate. Got any ideas?"

Tony: "Gonzo Ralph was sired by Crazy Eddy out of Missy Day, an Aussie broodmare I had Mrs. Murphy buy from a friend of mine in Melbourne. I sent Crazy Eddy to Australia to cover Missy Day's full sister, Missy Night. She drops a Gonzo lookalike, Crazy Ralph. The trouble is, the horse doesn't have what it takes; so my friend hasn't registered him."

Jesse: "Sounds promising, but can we get the horse, and how much will it cost us?"

Tony: "He's been trying to unload the horse for months, keeps sending me photographs asking if I can find a sucker who'll take him. We should be able to get him cheap, but we'll have to pay to have him transported. The genetics will be perfect, and we can tattoo him with Gonzo's number. We don't even have to fake the registration papers. What we need is a duplicate implant, just in case they get curious, but I doubt it, nobody gives a shit about losers. They only check the winners. I can have the horse sent up next week."

Jesse: "Good. Do it."

Lake: "But what about the physical switch?"

Tony: "Gonzo Ralph is in my barn. I got horses coming and going back and forth from the farm to the track all the time. The physical switch will be easy."

Jesse: "The Aussie Switch... I like it. I'll have my people lay the bets around the country so that nothing is suspected and our hands are clean. I'll look after Richard's end." She looks at Tony, "Let me know your costs and don't get cute, we'll straighten out when you bring me the cash for your bet. I'll look after the rest."

Lake: "Even if we pull this off, can we make any money on one race?"

Jesse: "Maybe, if a long shot wins our race, but that's not the point. Nobody fucks with my race-track."

**PAL-E HYEONGJE - BROTHERS IN ARMS**

# 9
## Pal-e Hyeongje - Brothers In Arms

Larry Dodd Sims is a busy boy, especially for someone who would rather play than work, but work he does, continuing in his roles as ITIF consultant and Chief Systems Analyst at Total Tote Systems. If that wasn't enough Sims continues working with Cisco cashing the near-expired uncashed winning tickets he's gleamed from Total Totes' servers. And in his spare time, he pursues his digital heist of SKE-Sport, securing his position as *Jeonja Kauboi*, amassing a small fortune of just over one million US dollars all sitting in a Seoul bank account under the name of Marcie Reynolds, Davey Cisco's ex-wife.

Of course neither Cisco nor his ex wife know anything about the bank account, or so Larry Dodd Sims thinks. If the *Pal-e Hyeongje* ever finds out Sims stole millions of dollars, he'd be dead in a week.

The solution was easy: create a digital trail that leads to someone else, a person associated with someone who has a history of shady dealings, Davey Cisco. When the time is right, Sims will hop on a plane to Seoul, find some nice cooperative dame looking to make a few bucks, and turn her into Marcie Reynolds in order to cash out. Creating a false identity for the bank will be child's play compared to all the other more sophisticated scams he's pulling. All systems are go. Once he collects his share of the Pick Six winnings, it's off to find his Seoul-mate, the pseudo Marcie Reynolds.

Jesse sits in Johnny Luck's office discussing the latest developments involving the ITIF and her plan on how they're going to screw Johansson and Sims.

Luck: "It's a lot of wheeling and dealing just to screw a couple of assholes."

Jesse: "We could make a few bucks on the race."

Luck: "Pocket change, hardly worth the trouble."

Jesse: "I don't like people screwing with my race-tracks. They need to be taught a lesson. If these clowns are allowed to get away with this Pick Six bullshit, god knows the damage Sims could do."

Luck: "I could just pick up the phone and call Total Tote, I know the President."

Jesse: "And they'd call the FBI, and the next thing we know, we got Feds crawling up our ass. Is that what you want?" Luck doesn't answer; he knows she's right.

Jesse: "Besides, you haven't heard the latest, I have the identity of the second Yankee fan in the ticket cashing fiddle. We caught his face on camera as he was leaving the grandstand. It's Larry Dodd Sims. He must be using his position at Total Tote to duplicate all the uncashed winning tickets."

Luck's secretary buzzes, "It's Mr. Yeung on line three." Johnny picks up the phone, "Good morning Benson, how are you feeling?" Benson Yeung is the Hong Mian Dragon Head, Johnny Luck's boss. "Yes sir, of course, no problem at all. Jesse? She's with me right now. Of course, we'll both give him our full co-operation." Johnny smiles, "Yes sir, I'll tell her." He hangs up.

Jesse: "What's up?"

Luck: "We have an out-of-town guest on his way to see us. He'll be here any minute. We're to show him full co-operation, and Benson wants you to be polite."

Jesse: "Polite, I'm always polite."

Luck: "Really, since when?"

Before Jesse can defend herself, Lucks' secretary enters, "There's a Colonel Park and associate here to see you. Mr. Yeung sent him."

Colonel Lee-Sam Park (Ret.) is a high-ranking member of the *Pal-e Hyeongje.* Park and his bodyguard enter Lucks' office. Park introduces himself and takes a seat in the chair beside Jesse.

The bodyguard stands silent behind him and off to the side.

Park: "It's a pleasure to meet you. Mr. Yeung speaks very highly of both of you. He assured me that you can assist me in resolving a small problem with one of your clients."

Luck: "Of course Colonel Park, how can we be of service?"

Park: "As I am sure you know our organization has many interests as do you and Mr. Yeung. One of these interests is in an e-sport gambling company, SKE-Sport. Over the past year, we've found that one particular client has amassed a rather significant amount of winnings, an amount that would seem unlikely considering the safeguards built into the game... if you follow my meaning."

Jesse: "You mean you've been hacked." Luck gives Jesse a look, reminding her of Benson Yeung's instructions... be co-operative and polite. Park gives Jesse a smile.

Park: "Yes Miss James, hacked by *Jeonja Kauboi*, at least that's her *Dunoe Segseu* handle."

Luck: "*Dunoe Segseu?*"

Park: "It's a game. This so-called *Jeonja Kauboi*, only plays the big money games, the *Keun Sigan*, but the thing is, she wins. Of course players win occasionally, but her record is... unrealistic. In fact, it's impossible based on how the game is designed."

Jesse: "You mean it's rigged." Again Johnny shoots Jesse a warning look. Park turns to Jesse.

Park: "Well Miss James, I guess you could say our game is as honest as horse racing. Call it rigged, fixed, stacked, or whatever you like. The fact is, *Jeonja Kauboi* is a cheat, and in our business as in yours, cheating is a one-way street. Punishment must be meted out, and a message must be sent to anyone else thinking of interfering in our enterprise."

Jesse: "Of course, you have no choice."

Park: "I knew you'd understand. In any case, Mr. Yeung has sanctioned our operation."

Luck: "How can we help? You said this *Jeonja Kauboi* is a woman."

Park: "Well... yes and no. When we tracked the money, we found that the winnings are deposited into an account in the SIB Bank in Seoul. The owner of the account is an Australian expatriate who lives in Macau, a Marcie Reynolds. She's an executive at one of the casinos. When we contacted Miss Reynolds, she knew nothing of the account. Of course we didn't identify ourselves. Our man pretended to be a SIB Investment Counselor, suggesting the funds should be more productively employed, but she assured us we were mistaken. She insisted, the account holder must be another Marcie Reynolds.

When we checked further, we found Miss Reynolds never played *Dunoe Segseu* and didn't even know what it was, so we checked for relatives and associates. It turns out Miss Reynolds has an ex husband, and when we traced IP records, we found her ex husband was in fact the *Jeonja Kauboi*."

Jesse: "And who is Marcie Reynolds ex hubby?"

Park: "David Cisco, I believe he's a trainer that works out of the Hancock Racetrack." Warning sirens start going off in Jesse's head.

Luck: "Go ahead Jesse, tell him."

Jesse explains that Davey Cisco and his twin bother, Pauley, are both trainers at the Hancock. Pauley left Australia so he could distance himself from his more flamboyant brother who was constantly getting suspended for various offences; eventually Davey wore out his welcome Down Under. He followed his brother to LA, and they both ended up at the Hancock.

Although Pauley tends to keep his nose clean, Davey continued to get involved in various nefarious schemes, one of which was a ticket cashing scam. His partner in the ticket cashing operation is a computer consultant and gambler, Larry Dodd Sims. Both men are also partners in ITIF, another of their questionable business enterprises. Jesse goes on to describe how she infiltrated the ITIF, which has led to some very interesting intelligence, some of which did not seem relevant until today.

Jesse: "It seems that Sims has been bragging to his partners at ITIF how he's hacked some South Korean e-sport company, and that he's beat them for over a million bucks. Of course we had no idea this gaming company was one of yours."

Park: "So Sims and Cisco are partners in your ticket cashing scam, and apparently also in the *Dunoe Segseu* hack.

Luck: "It seems to be the case."

Park: "I assume you have no objections to having my associate, Mr. Kim, cleanup both outstanding issues." Jesse and Luck look at Park's bodyguard who bows ever so slightly.

**CRAZY RALPH**

# 10
# Crazy Ralph

Truffatore has been using a non-traditional training regiment for Gonzo Ralph. The traditional training method calls for long, slow gallops designed to build strength in the tendons and bones. The 'leg up' process as it is called, employs a system of slowly increasing the training distance to two miles at a pace of eighteen to twenty seconds/furlong. Breezes of between one to four furlongs are added every seven to ten days at a pace of thirteen seconds/furlong.

Unfortunately, research suggests this may not be the best method of protecting thoroughbreds from a repetitive loading injury to their shins. This so called traditional method develops what trainers call 'gallop' bone rather than 'breeze' bone, the physiology required for a racehorse to sustain a racing career.

The modified method employs shorter gallops of between a mile and a mile and a quarter ending in a breeze of three furlongs in forty seconds. This is the training regiment Truffatore uses. The bottom line is simple, Gonzo Ralph is in excellent racing condition, but the method is controversial, and some trainers believe it's worse than the traditional training procedure. Jesse figures she can use this controversy to her advantage. If Sims is able to fix the Pick Six ticket, it's unlikely pulling the Aussie switch will make any difference; perhaps a Plan B is in order.

On one of Jesse's routine visits to shed row, she casually runs into Gonzo's jockey, The Pope, John Paul, an old friend from her racing days. She pulls John Paul aside to give him instructions. Jesse's plan is to feign a Gonzo Ralph injury, putting in doubt the horse's ability to race effectively in the Mogul Invitational.

Other trainers, including Davey Cisco, a couple of jockey agents, and a few reporters are all standing by the rail watching the morning workouts in preparation for the upcoming Mogul Invitational.

While Truffatore supervises the groom saddling Gonzo Ralph, Jesse talks to John Paul.

Jesse: "John, I want you to keep Gonzo at a fifteen second pace for two furlongs, then we need a show. Pretend to ask him to give you all he's got, but keep him at fifteen, then pull-up like something's wrong. Jump off and check his leg. Tony will run out to see what's happened. Tell him the horse didn't feel right when you asked him to go and look worried. Point to his shin. I want the rail jockeys to think he's hurt."

John Paul: "Is Tony in on this?"

Jesse: "Better he doesn't know. Anybody asks, tell them it's nothing, but don't act convinced. When they press you about it, grumble about Tony's training procedure, and how it hasn't built-up Gonzo's 'breeze' bone. You're afraid under the stress of a big race the horse will breakdown, but make it all hush-hush. The more you tell people to keep it to themselves, the more they'll spread the rumor. It's human nature. Got it."

John Paul: "Sure, no problem. Just put a few bucks on him for me when the time comes."

Jesse: "Don't I always look after my friends?"

John Paul: "Consider it done Jesse. Gary Stevens ain't the only jock that can act. I'll have those rail jockeys flapping their gums like teenage girls with a hot date. By the time I'm done, they'll think Gonzo is finished."

Jesse and John Paul make their way over to Gonzo Ralph. Truffatore helps John Paul up onto the horse. Jesse turns to Truffatore. "Is Crazy Ralph at the farm?"

Truffatore: "He arrived the day before yesterday. It's amazing, they're dead ringers. No one could tell them apart by just looking."

Jesse: "After John Paul does his thing. Load Gonzo Ralph up and take him out to your farm. Anyone asks, you just want him to rest up a few days. You'll make the switch at the farm and bring them both back. When you breeze Crazy Ralph as

Gonzo, his times will be slow. Anybody asks, you're saving him for the big race."

Truffatore: "What if somebody asks about Crazy Ralph?"

Jesse: "Tell them you're just evaluating him for a potential buyer. Nothing special."

Truffatore: "This seems like a lot of trouble with little return, if you ask me."

Jesse: "Did I fucking ask you?"

Truffatore shakes his head and heads for the rail to clock Gonzo Ralph. Everything goes as planned. John Paul keeps Gonzo to a mediocre pace despite acting like he's calling for speed. When Gonzo Ralph gets to just where the rail jockeys are standing he pulls him up and jumps off with a concerned look on his face. Truffatore runs out onto the track. John Paul puts on an award-winning performance. Truffatore looks very concerned, he looks up to find Jesse, but she's gone.

By lunchtime the word is out, Gonzo Ralph is hurt, he may not be able to compete in the Mogul Invitational, his career could be over. The vets have been called in to determine if he can ever race again. It's all nonsense of course, but it doesn't take much to start a rumor at the race-track.

## THE PICK SIX

# 11
## The Pick Six

Sims, Johansson, and Cisco meet for coffee at The Cheesecake Factory in a mall only a few blocks from The Hancock Complex. Johansson looks at Sims who's whittling away on an enormous piece of cheesecake covered in bright red strawberry topping, dripping down the sides like blood oozing from an open wound. Davey Cisco is eyeballing one of the pretty waitresses in her neat white shirt and black tie, all tightly wrapped in a crisp white apron like a virginal package waiting to be opened.

Johansson: "If we're going all-in on this, I want to know how it works."

Sims: "All you have to do is place the bets. We need to pick the winners for all six races in the Pick Six, including the Mogul Invitational."

Cisco's attention is focused on the pretty waitress. Sims is agitated at Cisco's lack of interest. He turns to Cisco, "Davey! For Christ sake, stop flirting with the broad and pay attention to the plan."

Cisco: "I know how a Pick Six works."

Sims: "Pay attention, anyway."

Cisco: "Fine, I'm listening."

Sims: "For the first four races you can bet any horse. There's a delay in the system of about twenty minutes, that gives me time to get into the system, find the records for our tickets, change the numbers, and print out corrected versions, There's not enough time to fix the last two races, so the safest thing to do is bet on all the horses in those races. That means we have to buy twenty-six tickets so we're covered."

Johansson: "I heard from Lake, there's something wrong with Gonzo Ralph. His workout times were lousy after his jockey pulled him up. The word is, he's not fit to race and could breakdown. There's definitely something wrong with him. Truffatore is worried. Maybe we shouldn't waste a ticket on him? Why bet on a horse that can't win?"

Sims: "It doesn't matter, we bet all the horses in the last two races. Think of it as insurance. I don't trust Truffatore. He's far too cozy with Lake, and he's got a history with that Jesse James broad, and she's bad news. Besides, if we don't bet on our own horse somebody will smell a rat."

Davey: "He's right Jimmy, betting all the horses in the last two races is the smart move."

Johansson: "So we place our bets as suggested and dump the company pool on Gonzo Ralph to win. If he wins, the company gets a big payday; if he loses, the company goes tits-up, but at that point, who cares, we'll have our payday. It's all coming together, this is our exit plan."

**JESSE'S MOVE**

# 12
## Jesse's Move

Jesse is in her office stretched out on her couch watching David Cronenberg's horror classic, *Dead Ringer* starring Jeremy Irons. She looks at her watch, its 2:15 AM; it's time. She gets up, leaves her office, and heads for shed row.

It's dark, and the place is deserted except for one elderly security guard asleep on a lawn chair. As she approaches the old man, he wakes up.

"Evening Jesse, beautiful night. Anything wrong?"

Jesse: "Nothing serious Pops. Just taking a walk. Thought I'd tell my troubles to the horses, they're good listeners."

Pops: "That they are my dear, that they are, but what kind of troubles could a pretty young thing like you get into?"

Jesse: "Oh, I'm full of surprises."

Pops: "I'll bet you are?"

Jesse takes some cash out of her pocket and hands it to Pops. "Do me a favor Pops. Stroll on down to the coffee machine by the entrance and get me a coffee, extra cream, no sugar."

Pops looks at the cash in his hand. He's holding five twenty-dollar bills. "You sure you just want a coffee, there's enough here for a Danish… from Denmark."

Jesse smiles and kisses the old man on his stubbled cheek. "Take your time Pops, and while you're at it, you can drink that coffee and partake in a Danish or two if the mood strikes."

Pops gives Jesse an animated stage wink and shuffles off down shed row towards the coffee machine near the entrance. Jesse watches as the old man disappears into the blackness, his bent outline periodically illuminated by the lights along the footpath.

Once he disappears Jesse moves to the barn where Gonzo Ralph has been placed. There's a hand-painted cardboard sign labeled "Crazy Ralph" nailed onto the stall door. The stall beside it has a fancy wooden name plaque announcing it's the home of "Gonzo Ralph," but in fact, its current occupant is Crazy Ralph.

Everything is working as planned. Gonzo Ralph was sent out to Truffatore's Anaheim horse farm where his double, Crazy Ralph, was enjoying the good life. When the horses were brought back to The Hancock, the switch was in place.  Earlier in the week, when Crazy Ralph was breezed as Gonzo Ralph, his times were mediocre, confirming around the track that Gonzo wasn't fit. The odds in the Vegas books started to climb, by Post Time, the odds-on-favorite only a week ago, would be a long shot.

Davey Cisco and his pals were well aware of Gonzo Ralph's problems, but the Pick Six didn't rely on him winning. If Gonzo became a long shot and won, the payoff would be huge, even if the five other winners were all favorites. Any long shot winner in any of the six races would mean big money, maybe as much as six or seven million dollars.

After the race the partners were to meet at the Clarence Motor Lodge, a second rate motel near the airport and across the road from the busiest off track betting parlor in LA. They had not decided on what to do next. Johansson wanted to sit on the ticket until the dust settled on the ITIF, but Cisco and Sims wanted to cash out immediately. If they sat on the ticket who was going to hold it? Trust amongst conmen is always in short supply.

As far as Jesse is concerned, let these clowns pull their digital heist. The Koreans would deal with Cisco and Sims, and one call to Mo Fields about Johansson would complete the lethal trifecta. If Jesse's plan works, the ITIF would be cash rich and controlled solely by Jesse's man, Richard Lake, and the Hong Mian would have another asset in their portfolio.

Jesse opens the stall door labeled Crazy Ralph and removes Gonzo. She ties him to a post. She then removes Crazy Ralph from Gonzo's stall and puts him in his proper barn. She then puts Gonzo Ralph back in his own stall. The double switch is complete. She looks down shed row and she sees Pops slowly making his way back to his lawn chair.

Jesse takes out her cell phone and hits the button marked 'The Pope.' The phone rings. John Paul answers. "John it's Jesse, sorry to wake you, but it's important. It's about the Mogul Invitational."

Jesse tells John Paul what she's done. He is to go for the win and ignore whatever instructions Truffatore gives him. Only Jesse and John Paul know that Gonzo Ralph is back in play. She hangs up and heads for where Pops has resumed his position in the lawn chair.

Pops: "Have a nice talk to the animals?"

Jesse: "You never know Pops. One day they may talk back."

Pops: "They'd only bitch about conditions. Probably want to form a union or some such shit."

Jesse: "Yeah you're probably right. Better they stay quiet."

Pops hands Jesse a coffee: "They didn't have any Danishes. You want your change?"

Jesse: "Nah, keep the change? Goodnight Pops." She starts to walk away.

Pops: "Hay Jesse… how's that English husband of your's?"

Jesse turns: "Out of town on business. Think I'd be talking to horses in the middle of the night if I had him to go home to?" She waves and keeps on walking.

**RACE DAY**

# 13
# Race Day

It's not just gambling that brings people out to the racetrack, it's ritual: the parade of exquisite animals, the brightly colored silks, the women in ridiculous headgear, calling them hats would be an insult to hats, and the hysterical antics of the rail-bums waving their two-dollar tickets in anticipation of a big score that never comes. Horse racing is pageantry, perhaps tragic opera where the super wealthy and the fabulously famous commingle with the great-unwashed, each participating in their own way in an ancient blood sport in pursuit of the unattainable. Circus Maximus lives.

Race day is full of ceremony, time-honored rites designed to protect the integrity of a sport that has none. It's not like it's a secret. Everyone knows jockeys use machines, hold horses, and take payoffs. Everyone knows the trainers play Russian roulette with their horse's health, and the vets are little more than drug pushers.

Everybody knows the fix is in more times than not, but in the end, it doesn't matter. For the betting public that populates the grandstand, it's the spectacle that turns their crank, but for insiders, it's about money.

Truffatore is at the track before the sun comes up. He checks to see that Crazy Ralph has eaten all his breakfast, not realizing Jesse has pulled the double switch, and that the horse in Gonzo Ralph's stall is in fact, Gonzo Ralph. He takes Gonzo's temperature and looks him over, checking to see if he'll pass the State Veterinarian's muster. He's surprised at the excellent shape the horse is in, since Crazy Ralph is actually a few months younger and not quite as mature as Gonzo.

When the vet arrives, he runs his hands down the horse's forelegs making sure there is no swelling or heat. The groom walks Gonzo back and forth in front of the stall so the official can watch for any obvious problems. Since the word is out that Gonzo is injured, the vet asks the groom to see Gonzo jog. He then checks the tattoo on the horse's inner lip and makes sure that it matches the horse's official Jockey Club Registration. He also does a cursory visual inspection looking for unique markings, making sure the horse described in the registration papers looks like the horse standing in front of him. Gonzo Ralph passes inspection with flying colors.

A little later in the morning one of the apprentice jockey's takes Gonzo for a light jog just to warm him up and loosen the muscles. At this point Gonzo, knows it's race day, and he starts to prepare mentally. They say horses have tiny brains, but they are athletes, and when the bell rings, the good ones will give you all they got.

After the light jog, the groom gives Gonzo a bath and muzzles him so he can't eat anymore feed. Since the Mogul Invitational is the sixth race on the card, Gonzo just waits. His jockey, John Paul, has a busier schedule; he's got four other rides on the day's card.

The Mogul Invitational is a mile and sixteenth race on a dirt track with a purse of two million dollars. The winner receives one million, three hundred thousand. Twenty minutes before post time, Gonzo and his competitors are called to the Receiving Barn for a final inspection. The Horse Inspector checks to see if the horseshoes are legal and the Horse Identifier does a second check of the tattoo and markings, making sure everything matches with the official registration papers. Once the inspection is complete Gonzo Ralph is taken to the saddling paddock where the Paddock Judge inspects all the gear, including saddle, bits, and blinkers. Gonzo is then saddled, does a couple of tours of the walking ring, then out to the track for a brief warm up on the way to the starting gate.

The assistant starters coax the twelve handsome two-year-olds and their brightly colored riders into the electronic starting gate. John Paul wears bright red silks with black arms, black collar, and a red and black helmet cover, the colors of

Peanut Spread Stables. His main competition is Not So Lazy, a classy looking red roan with good speed but little stamina.

The bell sounds and the horses leap from the starting gate like the Charge of the Light Brigade, but instead of being led by Lord Cardigan, Not So Lazy takes the lead.

The start of a horserace is the most dangerous time. All twelve horses are bunched together as they try to find their optimum position. Some horses go for the rail so they have less ground to cover while others stay in the middle trying to avoid getting boxed-in. Not So Lazy goes for the rail in an effort to cut the distance and maintain his sprinting advantage, minimizing his lack of stamina.

John Paul keeps Gonzo Ralph tucked neatly in fourth position as they make the first turn. By the time they reach the five-eighth pole on the back-stretch seven horses have fallen back. The front pack consists of Not So Lazy, Bad Dude, and Reilly, with Gonzo Ralph in fourth, three lengths back. By the time they hit the three-eights' pole, it's down to a three horse race: Not So Lazy is first, Bad Dude is second, and Gonzo Ralph is third, two lengths back. The rest of the field is no longer a factor.

As they come out of the Clubhouse turn past the quarter pole Gonzo Ralph has moved up, just one length back. Into the home stretch Not So Lazy starts to fade, it's Bad Dude first and Gonzo Ralph second. Both jockeys go to the whip. It's neck and neck. At the sixteenth pole Gonzo Ralph decides enough is enough. He charges for the finish line edging Bad Dude by half a length.

The Unofficial Finish goes up on the board: Gonzo Ralph first; Bad Dude second; and Not So Lazy third. There are no fouls. It's Official. Gonzo Ralph pays eighteen dollars, not bad for a horse that only a week earlier was an even money favorite. Thanks to the higher than expected odds on Gonzo Ralph and an unexpected long shot winning the third race, the Pick Six pays a record three million, seven hundred and forty-nine thousand dollars, and change.

**PAULEY CISCO**

# 14
## Pauley Cisco

Pauley Cisco arrives home from the track at about eight-thirty in the evening. He had a couple of horses running in the early races but nothing in the Mogul. He spends the rest of the day watching the races and placing a few bets.

He checks the phone in the kitchen and sees the message light flashing. He presses the Play button: "Pauley, it's me. I think I'm in trouble. Some Korean thug is following me. I've got to disappear."

It's happened again. It was only a matter of time before Davey got in over his head. Pauley knew Davey and his poker pals were trying something crazy with ITIF, and he knew Sims all too well. It's Sims the Koreans should be going after, not Davey. Pauley knew all about Sims SKE-Sport hack. He couldn't stop bragging how he beat them for a ton of dough. When he got involved in the uncashed ticket cashing scam with Sims, he knew the guy was reckless, but why go after Davey, unless they thought Davey was involved in the SKE scam with Sims, or worse, they mistook Davey for him. If the Koreans were getting rid of everyone involved with Sims, he'd be next.

Pauley isn't sure what to do. He stands there paralyzed trying to figure his next move. If Davey felt he had to disappear, his best option is to do the same. He had his exit strategy in place, now seemed like the right time to implement it. Davey is on his own, the further they separate the better for both of them. He'd grab his passport and some clothes and get his ass to the airport, then on to Macau and Marcie.

He notices the indentation of a phone number on the pad beside the kitchen phone. Davey must have written it down and taken the note. Pauley takes a pencil out of the drawer and lightly scribbles over the embossed marks revealing a local number he doesn't recognize. He dials the number, "Good evening, Clarence Motor Lodge, how can we be of service?"

Pauley: "Yes hello… I understand a friend of mine is staying at your motel, I wonder if you can tell me if he's arrived?"

Motel Manager: "Your friend's name?"

Pauley: "David Cisco."

Pauley can hear the Motel Manager leafing through some pages of an appointment book, "Sorry, we don't have a David Cisco staying with us."

Pauley: "How about a James Johansson?"

More pages ruffling: "No. No Johansson."

Pauley: "Maybe you've got a listing for Larry Sims?"

Motel Manager: "Mister, you sure got a lot of friends…"

Pauley: "It's a class reunion. You know how it is."

Motel Manager: "Been there…" There are more sounds of pages being turned. "Yeah…  Sims, he checked in yesterday but I haven't seen him around."

Pauley: "What room is he in."

Motel Manager: "Room 207, but I don't want any trouble: no broads or crazy stuff. I know how these college reunions can get. I had a Polish veterans convention once, practically destroyed the place. You're not one of them are you?"

Pauley: "Nah, just old fraternity brothers."

Motel Manager: "Got a funny accent for an American?"

Pauley: "Foreign student. Anyway, thanks for your help." He hangs up.

Pauley goes into the bedroom and opens the armoire. He rifles through a shelf stacked with sweaters. His passport is gone. Goddamn it! Davey took his passport in case he needed to switch identities. He's gone too far; Pauley had to get his passport back. Without it, he was screwed. He goes to the safe he had installed when he first moved in and finds his Colt 1911 Series 70 Semi Automatic. Pauley thinks to himself, 'This isn't going to end well.'

**ROOM 207**

# 15
# Room 207

Mo Fields has been patiently tailing Jimmy Johansson all day. He watched as Johansson and Sims ate lunch at a noodle joint near the track. It was curious that Cisco wasn't invited. It's not as if he had any horses on the card other than his interest in Gonzo Ralph, but Gonzo's trainer is Truffatore, so there was no reason why Cisco couldn't attend the party. Their lunchtime conversation was animated, almost heated, with Johansson finally getting Sims to go along with whatever he was pitching. Perhaps Johansson wanted to cut Cisco out of the Pick Six payoff; perhaps it was the other way around. Fields didn't care. Jesse said take care of Johansson; let the Korean deal with Cisco and Sims.

Jesse's inside man, Richard Lake, had all the ITIF phones tapped, so he knew they all planned to meet at the Clarence Motor Lodge to make the split. The motel was only a few blocks away from an OTB parlor where they could cash their winning ticket. Fields just had to wait for the right moment when he could take Johansson out.

While Fields follows Johansson, Kim follows Davey Cisco. Cisco gets to the track early and checks on his horses. Since he hasn't any of them running in the day's races he leaves, returning to his brother's condo, where he spends the balance of the day. Around seven o'clock in the evening Cisco leaves and goes to the Clarence Motor Lodge. Kim follows. When he gets to the motel, he parks his rented Ford Malibu, so he has a clear view of Room 207. Davey parks his truck beside an outdoor staircase that leads to a walkway and the rooms on the second floor. Kim sits trying to decide if he should just barge in and shoot Cisco or wait to see if Sims shows up. He figures he might as well wait for Sims; kill two pigeons with one rock, or whatever the silly English expression is.

As he waits, he sees a Cadillac pull into the parking lot and park right beside Cisco's truck. Kim flips open the manila file folder on the seat beside him. He shuffles through a half a dozen photographs until he finds the one that matches the man who just got out of the Caddie. It's James J. (Jimmy) Johansson. He watches as Johansson puts on a pair of gloves while looking in the back of Cisco's truck.

Johansson reaches into the truck and takes out some kind of power tool. It looks like an electric drill. What the hell are these guys going to do, build an ark for their escape? Johansson isn't on his list, he's the pretty blonde's problem, not his. Kim is a soldier, maybe he doesn't wear a uniform any more, but the Pal-e Hyeongje rules are the same, follow orders; do exactly as you are told; nothing more and nothing less. Colonel Park said he should eliminate the two men in the videos wearing Yankee baseball caps, period.

Johansson climbs the stairs and knocks on the door. The door opens and Johansson whacks Cisco in the head with the power tool. Interesting. Maybe half his job is done. Five minutes later Johansson exits Room 207. He walks down the staircase, dumps the power tool in the back of the truck and gets in his car.

Kim watches as a dark figure steps out from behind a garbage dumpster. There's a muzzle flash and the familiar sound of a suppressed gunshot. Jimmy Johansson slumps over onto the passenger seat disappearing from view. The dark figure raises his head in the direction of Kim. He knows he's been watching. It must be the pretty blonde's man, the guy they call, The Tailor. The figure disappears into the darkness.  Now what? The Clarence Motor Lodge is turning into a convention of hitmen.

Before Kim could decide whether to go up to Room 207 another car pulls into the parking lot. The guy driving is a dead ringer for Davey Cisco. It must be his brother. He heard Cisco had a twin. This was getting confusing, and seriously messy. The brother parks his car under a dim parking lot lamp that barely makes a dent in the darkness. He gets out of the car and heads for the staircase.

Pauley Cisco keeps one hand in his pocket as if he was holding a gun. He climbs the staircase and finds Room 207. He knocks on the door. No answer. He knocks again, still no answer. He tries to open the door. It opens. Pauley enters the darkened room to find the remains of his brother, head down on the motel room desk with a hole in his head made by what looks like Davey's own bolt driver. Pauley doesn't stick around long; he exits Room 207 and heads for his car. Pauley isn't on Kim's hit list. He lets him go.

Kim can't wait any longer. He has to find out what happened to Cisco. If Cisco is already dead, he really doesn't want to hang around much longer. His brother just might call the cops. Kim gets out of the car and heads for Room 207. The door is still unlocked. He enters. He turns on the light and sees Davey Cisco lying head down on the motel room desk. Kim walks over and lifts Cisco's head. He stares at the hole in his forehead. Interesting. No exit wound, no spent shell, no loud sound. He'd have to check out what that power tool was; it might come in handy one day. Kim stands in the middle of the room thinking; he better wait for Sims so he can complete the assignment. He hopes he arrives before housekeeping finds the body of the recently departed Davey Cisco, or there just might be some unfortunate collateral damage.

If Kim leaves now and Sims shows up to find Cisco's remains, he'll disappear, and that will make Colonel Park extremely angry, creating a situation that could end badly for Kim. A decision is made. He'll head back to his car and wait as long as possible. If Sims hasn't shown up before the motel maid starts making her rounds, he'll take-off; otherwise, he'll wait.

He leaves Room 207 and takes the stairs down to the parking area where he plans to wait for Sims in his car. He gets to the bottom of the staircase and heads for his car. As he does, he spots a darkened figure wearing a baseball cap walking towards him. As the figure passes under a parking lot light, he sees it's a Yankee cap. He turns toward the figure and reaches under his jacket for his Glock. He takes the suppressor out of his jacket pocket and screws it onto the end of the semi automatic.

The man stops as he sees what Kim is doing. He turns and starts to run. He gets about five yards. As he passes under the parking lot light Kim fires. The man tumbles forward and falls face-down on the asphalt. Kim goes to where the man is lying. He uses his foot to turn him over. The Yankee baseball cap is covering most of his face. There are gurgling noises coming from under the hat. Kim fires his two more times: once in the chest and once through the Yankee logo where the man's forehead should be.

Kim crouches down on his haunches. He uses his Glock to push the baseball cap off the man's head, revealing the face of the now deceased Larry Dodd Sims. Kim smiles, his job is complete,

Sims and Cisco are both dead. He figures he deserves a reward; perhaps Sims is caring some cash. He checks his pockets and finds a ticket from The Hancock Racetrack. If Sims kept it, it must be a winner. Kim is very pleased with himself as he ponders what the value of the winning ticket is.

The sound of what could have been a car backfiring is heard by the Motel Manager and some residents, but it's not. In fact, it's the sound of Pauley Cisco's Colt semi automatic. The bullet goes through the back of Kim's head and comes out the other side with a substantial amount of brain matter splattering all over the parking lot asphalt. Kim falls forward onto Larry Dodd Sims still holding the winning Pick Six ticket.

Pauley Cisco had been quietly waiting in his car watching the events unfold. He knew Sims would show up eventually with the winning ticket. As far as he was concerned, it was compensation for the death of his brother. He was surprised Kim didn't notice he never left the parking lot after visiting Room 207. When he saw Sims arrive, he got out of his car to follow but stopped when he saw Kim coming down the motel staircase. He waited to see what would happen. As things worked out Kim did his job for him. Pauley looks down at the two bodies one piled on top of the other. He bends down and takes the Pick Six ticket from Kim's hand.

"Drop the gun and hand me the ticket." Mo Fields steps out from behind the motel dumpster. "I'd do what I'm told if I was you. I still have a few bullets left in my piece."

Pauley drops his gun. "Who are you?"

Fields: "I'm your guardian angel." Fields steps forward and takes the ticket.

Pauley: "You're not going to kill me?"

Fields: "For cashing uncashed tickets with your pal, Sims... Nah, I don't think so. Besides, my job was Johansson, not you, but you really should disappear. In a few hours, the cops will be all over this place and they'll sure as hell be looking for you, especially being a foreigner and all."

Pauley: "Can I go?"

Fields: "Yeah you can go, and take your piece with you, but get rid of it before you takeoff for Macau and your brother's ex."

In a few hours Pauley would be on a plane to Macau. Screw the wrong people and you're likely to find yourself on the wrong side of green grass. Davey was always reckless, always a pain in the ass, always getting both of them in trouble, now he's dead. It was only a matter of time. He didn't get the Pick Six bonanza, but he still had the cash from the uncashed ticket scam, and he still had

Marcie and access to Sims' SKE-Sport winnings, still sitting in a Seoul bank account under Marcie's name.

**NOT QUITE THE END**

## 16
## Not Quite The End

Jesse and her husband, William Stone, lay in bed naked. Stone arrived earlier in the evening from an extended business trip to Hong Kong, Macau, and Seoul. He can't sleep; he's still on Seoul time. The condo buzzer sounds. He turns his head to look at his wife. She's sound asleep.  Stone forces his weary body out of bed. He slips on a black kimono he picked up while in Hong Kong. He walks to the front entrance. The buzzer sounds two more times.

Stone presses the speaker. "Yes…"

Doorman: "There's a Mr. Fields here to see Mrs. Stone."

Stone: "What's he look like?"

Doorman: "About forty, well dressed…"

Stone: "Okay, send him up." Stone goes into the kitchen and gets a glass of water. There's a knock on the door. He goes to the door and opens its.

Fields: "Evening Will, been on a trip?"

Stone looks at his luggage that is still sitting by the door where he dropped it when he got home. Jesse couldn't wait to tear his clothes off. He was more than willing to comply despite the jet lag. "Yeah, just got back early this evening. You want to come in?"

Fields has an envelope in his hand: "No it's okay, I'm just dropping this off for Jesse." He shows Stone the envelope. "Is she around?"

Stone: "She's asleep."

Fields: "Give her this." He hands Stone an envelope embossed with the Three Kings logo on the front. Stone looks inside. It's a ticket from the Hancock Racetrack.

Fields: "You should drop by the shop, I got some nice new material from Italy that just came in."

Stone: "Sounds good, I'll come by some time this week."

Fields: "Make sure Jesse gets that as soon as she wakes up." Stone nods and closes the door.

**SEOUL, SOUTH KOREA**

# 17
## Seoul, South Korea

As Pauley stepped off the airplane at the Incheon International Airport in Seoul, he felt a sense of excitement. He's traveling light, just a small carry-on with some toiletries and a change of clothes. There was no time to worry about packing; things were moving too fast. With Sims' SKE-Sport winnings and the money he made on the ticket cashing scam he could afford a new wardrobe and a nice extended vacation. The priority was getting the hell out of LA before the Koreans caught up to him although he really didn't know if they were even looking. If they were, hanging around Seoul might not be too smart, but he needed to get his hands on Sim's winnings, and besides, hiding right in front of their noses may be the smartest move of all.

In any case, he had nothing to do with Sims' SKE-Sport hacking. His association with Sims was limited to the uncashed ticket cashing hustle, and that really didn't harm anybody. Sure Sims hacked Total Tote, but the tickets were real winners, so the cash being paid out didn't affect them or the Hancock Racetrack. Total Tote and that James woman might be pissed, but would they really kill him when they didn't lose a dime. If you think about it, he and Sims did Total Tote a favor by bringing their attention to a hole in their security. Of course that's just a rationalization, but true nevertheless; besides, they may not even know about it yet. If the Chinese gangsters that run the Hancock wanted him dead, he'd be dead; or else the guy in the Clarence Motor Lodge parking lot wouldn't have let him off the hook.

On the other hand, he did blow the brains of that Korean thug all over the asphalt of Clarence Motor Lodge parking lot. That surely wouldn't be taken lightly, but did anybody but the other hitman know? Like the guy said, his job was to eliminate Johansson, period, but somebody must be pissed off, so it's probably a good idea to meet Marcie, collect the dough stashed in the SIB Bank, and get the hell out of South Korea as quickly as possible.

Pauley doesn't need to collect any luggage, so he goes directly to customs. They ask a few routine questions showing little interest in his arrival, just another Aussie looking for a good time and some Asian entertainment. Marcie is waiting as he comes through customs. They kiss and head straight for a waiting taxicab, then on to the hotel where they reacquaint themselves with each other's body in a greatly anticipated romantic reunion. Tomorrow they'd be at the SIB Bank as soon as it opened; they'd transfer the winnings to the Macau Commercial Bank where the money from the ticket cashing scam waits.

The following morning Pauley and Marcie get up, have breakfast, and take a cab to the SIB Bank located in the historical Jung District in the heart of Seoul. The area maintains some of the architecture and flavor of old Seoul by integrating traditional cultural landmarks with the steel, glass and concrete functionality required of a modern international business center.

When Pauley and Marcie arrive at the bank, they ask to speak to a manager concerning their account. The teller checks their account and tells them someone from the executive suite will help them. Pauley was hoping to get some low level flunky that would just do what they wanted, unfortunately when the teller saw the seven-figure plus balance, he figured he better get one of the big shots to handle the transaction, especially since the client wasn't a Korean. After about five minutes an attractive young woman arrives to escort Pauley and Marcie to a private elevator that can only be accessed with a digital fingerprint scan. They take the elevator up to the twenty-fifth floor. When they step off the elevator, their feet sink into a two-inch thick wool carpet; they are struck with the noiseless environment that belies the wheeling and dealing that is happening behind closed doors.

They are ushered into a large boardroom with the longest boardroom table either one has ever seen. They are seated at the far end facing the window that overlooks downtown Seoul. The place reeks of money and power. The amount in their account is substantial, but it hardly warrants this kind of attention. The high-powered scrutiny makes Pauley nervous. They wait.

Five minutes later another young woman arrives delivering a tray of tea. She doesn't say a word. She just places the tea down at the opposite end of the boardroom table. She pours four cups, leaving two at the window end of the table. She delivers the other two to where Pauley and Marcie are sitting.

Pauley: "Excuse me… but who exactly are we waiting for?"

The woman doesn't say a word. She just bows, turns, and leaves. Fifteen minutes pass. Marcie looks at Pauley, "This isn't normal, something is wrong. Maybe we should leave." Before Pauley can answer, two men arrive along with the woman that brought them up to the twenty-fifth floor.

The older gentleman is short, has thick white hair, is about sixty-five-years-old, and expensively dressed in a conservative, but elegant, navy blue pinstriped suit. He sits at the end of the table. The other man is taller, slim, about fifty-five-years-old, and equally well dressed, sporting a vertically striped Turnbull & Asser tie and a custom white shirt to go along with his charcoal grey Savile Row suit.

The woman speaks, "We apologize for the delay but we are waiting for two people that arrived early this morning from LA. They are on their way up now."

Pauley: "I don't understand the need for this meeting, all we want to do is transfer Miss Reynolds funds to her Macau bank account."

The woman smiles a noncommittal smile, "Please, enjoy your tea while we wait."

Pauley: "Well can you at least tell me who these gentlemen are?"

Female Bank Executive: "This is Mr. Shinn, President of the SIB Bank and this is Colonel Lee-Sam Park, the man your partner stole from, and Mr. Kim's superior, the man you killed in the Clarence Motor Lodge parking lot. Pauley goes stone cold white. Marcie feels faint. Shinn and Park simultaneously raise their cups and take a sip of tea as if it is some choreographed ritual preceding something far more deadly. Before their cups are returned to their saucers Jesse James and her husband William Stone are ushered into the room. More tea is served.

Jesse takes a sip of her tea. She looks at Pauley: "You really didn't think you'd get away with this, did you?"

**LOOSE ENDS**

## Part Three

## 18
## Loose Ends

This is the end of the story of the Aussie Switch, except life just doesn't stop because you've come to the end of a story, it continues in its normally mundane, repetitive routines until the day when the lights go out for good. So the question you must be asking yourself is, do the lights go out for Pauley Cisco and Marcie Reynolds, and why are Jesse and William Stone at this meeting?

Have faith, all will be revealed, but first we need to go back before the beginning, because like the end that really isn't the end, the beginning wasn't really the beginning.

### Marcie Reynolds

Before Pauley Cisco moved to Los Angeles, he lived in Sydney enjoying the bachelor life. Both Pauley and Davey trained horses and were partners in the Cisco Stud Farm And Stables on the outskirts of Sydney. The company was perpetually short of cash despite having the reputation as a quality breeder and trainer of racehorses.

Marcie worked as Vice President of Client Services for King's Garden Entertainment LLC, a casino operator in Sydney with wide-ranging interests including ownership of the Royal Court Racecourse where the Cisco brothers raced most of their horses as well as the horses they trained for other owners.

The financial and management stress of running the farm fell mostly on Pauley's shoulders. Add to that, Davey's habit of pushing the limits of the rules of the New South Wales Turf Club resulted in constant arguments between the two brothers. Davey's relationship with Marcie wasn't much better. His repeated suspensions from the track and his involvement with numerous shady underworld characters did not go down well with King's Garden management who needed to be cognizant of maintaining their lucrative gambling licenses.

Marcie's frequent business trips to Hong Kong and Macau added to the strain on their marriage, eventually resulting in divorce, but as much as couples want to find something different, they seem to seek comfort in the arms of lovers that are invariably carbon copies of the baggage they just shed. And so Marcie Reynolds found herself involved with Pauley Cisco, a similar but upgraded version of her ex husband, Davey.

King's Garden, like the Hancock, is owned by a consortium of interests hidden behind a tangled web of numbered companies and false fronts that stand in for Benson Yeung's Hong Mian and Colonel Lee-Sam Park's Pal-e Hyeongje. The actual operation of the casino is left to local partners who are responsible to the consortium. The KG Group's reach extends from Mainland China, Hong Kong and Seoul to Macau, Sydney, and Melbourne. Benson Yeung, the Hong Mian Dragon Head, survived and prospered because, like Meyer Lansky, he believed in alliances. In the US, the Hong Mian partnered with the Fungo Crime Family out of Buffalo and the Montoya Cartel in Mexico. In Asia, he partnered with the Pal-e Hyeongje based in Seoul, South Korea. In Europe, his associations are less formal, with working friendships, intelligence sharing, and tacit co-operation with clandestine elements of MI6.

King's Garden Casino caters primarily to high rollers: mostly corrupt government officials from Mainland China. This is in addition to the regular gaming profits earned from the Aussie locals and the commissions from laundering millions of narco-dollars. As VP of Client Services, Marcie Reynolds, an extremely attractive and well educated woman of thirty, was responsible for making sure clients were well looked after, providing luxury suites, gourmet food, expensive booze, exotic women, and recreational pharmaceuticals; whatever clients desired, as long as they generated their quota of rolling chip turnover.

But Marcie had a second job, as head of recruitment for MDP Excursions, a junket operation owned by Marcie, her ex-husband, and her current lover. It's one thing to get a divorce; it's another to unravel a spider web of business arrangements. The junket venture was the brain-child of William Stone, the financial, stock market, and money-laundering expert for the Hong Mian and the loving husband of ex jockey and current racetrack and gaming executive Jesse James. MDP Excursions was just one of several companies that delivered Mainland Chinese high rollers to Australian casinos operated by the KG consortium.

Getting Chinese citizens to gamble is easy. The Chinese people love to gamble. Walk down any side street in Hong Kong and you can hear the clicking of Mahjong tiles as they are slapped down on a table to a chorus of colorful Cantonese obscenities. The problem is not getting people to go on these excursions, that's the easy part. The problem is getting large amounts of cash out of China, and secondly, collecting the substantial losses incurred, usually money skimmed from business transactions or kickbacks on government contracts. This is where Stone's financial genius comes in to play.

Macau was the traditional hotbed destination for Chinese gamblers to feed their addictions, however, since the People's Republic of China took over the former Portuguese colony, the rules and their enforcement have been tightened. This government crackdown became more than a mere nuisance; it became downright dangerous; and so Australia became the next best pleasure destination for those Chinese officials eager to blow off some steam, as well as, substantial quantities of former government *Yuan*.

Marcie Reynolds subcontracted initial recruitment to a company that specialized in running a crew of exotic beauties who were instructed to steer corrupt Mainland Chinese government officials and wealthy businessmen to the King's Garden Casino. The gamblers were offered extensive luxury perks, as well as unlimited 'non-negotiable chips.' These VIP high rollers were given as many of these chips as they wanted. The junket operator got a commission on the volume of these chips lost by the clients they delivered to the casino; that is what is referred to as 'rolling chip turnover.'

If a player wins, they are paid out in what are called 'cash chips' that can be turned into cash held in the client's casino account, or they can be turned into more non-negotiable chips that can be used to gamble. In the long run, players lose whatever they've won, plus substantially more. It is the nature of gamblers to lose; psychologists might even argue, deep down, these addicts don't want to win.

If clients don't pay it's the junket operator that is responsible for collecting the money. If they can't collect, the debt becomes the responsibility of the junket operator; it's one reason the Cisco Stud Farm was constantly short of cash.

Since gambling losses are legally uncollectible in China, collecting debts can get tricky. You do not want to owe substantial amounts of money to the Hong Mian and their Pal-e Hyeongje partners.

As a consequence, junket operators like Marcie Reynolds and the Cisco brothers, contract collections to underworld characters that use whatever means is necessary to collect. Threats and blackmail are usually enough to get the job done, but on occasion, more extreme measures are required. Marcie's recruitment subcontractor and collection expert was a Hong Kong pimp and thug named Duke Feng.

**THE CHINESE CONNECTION**

# 19
## The Chinese Connection

It has been said China is ungovernable. Its current economic and military power belies the fact that in many ways it is still largely unmanageable, despite and maybe because of its roughly fifty million civil servants occupying eleven levels of government, consisting of twenty-seven ranks, divided into fourteen grades, all determining one's influence, status, responsibility, and benefits. During the Tang Dynasty (A.D. 618-907) there was one civil servant per two thousand, nine hundred and twenty-seven people. Over the years bureaucratic bloat expanded almost as much as the population. By the end of the Qin Dynasty (1644-1911) there was one official for every two hundred and ninety-nine citizens.

Today that ratio has exploded to one official for every twenty-seven people. If the United States followed the same governing pattern, the civil service would be substantially larger than it is. Perhaps all the people yelling for less government should be thankful for the efficiencies that do exist in Western democracies.

With a country as large, populous, and diverse as the People's Republic of China it is almost impossible to micro manage things on a local level.

There is a Chinese saying that goes back to the Yuan Dynasty (1206-1368): *the mountains are high, and the emperor is far away*, a more elegant turn of phrase than, *when the cat's away, the mouse will play.* A condition that is certain to ultimately lead local politicians to play loose and fast with easy access to government funds.

One of Marcie Reynolds' clients, a libidinous bureaucratic mouse by the name of Sammy Shen, liked to play high-stakes baccarat.

Sammy Shen, as he was known in Australia, was a high-ranking party official and civil servant in a prosperous Northern prefecture-level city. Shen was responsible for issuing municipal construction contracts, none of which ever got signed without some kickback, payoff, or benefit ending up in Sammy's very deep pockets.

The pressure of government service and corruption required some kind of release. And so Sammy Shen became a prized MDP client; a man with an abundance of funds at his disposal, and a fondness for the Punto Banco version of baccarat. As a consequence, Shen became a frequent guest of the King's Garden Casino and Royal Court Racecourse, delivered in luxury by MDP Excursions.

Of course Marcie Reynolds didn't deal directly with the clients until they arrived at the King's Garden Casino in Sydney; she relied on men like

Duke Feng, who ran the euphemistically named Duke's Executive Agency; a high end escort service ran out of a Kowloon office tower, only a short walk from the famous Peninsula Hotel. The rendezvous location where Sammy Shen often enjoyed the benefits of Duke's exotic executives. After a brief overnight stay at the Peninsula, enjoying the company of one of Duke's prettier employees, it was on to Sydney where Sammy spent his afternoons at the racetrack and his evenings at the baccarat table.

**THE WINNING STREAK**

## 20
## The Winning Streak

Shen, like most gamblers, was a consistent loser, however his constant flow of under the table cash always managed to be enough to cover his losses. He was also very superstitious, and if his luck turned bad, he'd switch from baccarat to blackjack or maybe even roulette. If things continued to go south, he'd threaten to move his business to another casino, and that was definitely not acceptable to KG or Marcie Reynolds, who as junket operator was responsible for Sammy's losses, as well as reimbursement of the cost of all the lavish perks the casino provided.

In order to forestall this eventuality, Marcie introduced Shen to her ex husband and current lover, Davey and Pauley Cisco. When things went badly at the tables, Sammy would head for the track where he'd search out Davey or Pauley, he never could tell the difference, in order to get some inside information on the days best bets.

On one auspicious afternoon Shen found Pauley, although he kept calling him Davey; Pauley suggested he might want to take a shot with one of his under-appreciated horses that would be going off at very favorable odds.

Shen figured his luck was about to turn so he decides to bet ten thousand dollars on a trifecta in the fourth race with Cisco's long-shot entry slotted to win and two other semi long shots to place and show. The result was a winning ticket worth four point eight million dollars. Shen immediately took his winnings and deposited them in his King's Garden Casino account. Two million went directly into King's Garden side of the ledger in order to payoff existing losses. That left Sammy with two point eight million dollars to play with, but before he returned to the tables he decided to celebrate with a hostess provided to him by Marcie Reynolds.

The young woman, Pansy Ping, was exotic, beautiful, and sexy, but she did not stop talking except for a brief time when her mouth was busy performing her assigned duties. When she was finished, she resumed her Mandarin chatter. Normally this would irritate Shen, but he had been working on a plan, and Pansy was about to become unwittingly part of the scheme.

Shen didn't become a senior bureaucrat because he was stupid despite what the casino executives thought. To them Shen was just another fool gambling away the illegal funds he managed to steal as Director of Infrastructure in his home town, a gamble as dangerous as fucking with the casino. But Shen was inventive in his illegal endeavors, and so he researched how to manipulate the odds at the baccarat table so that they would be in his favor.

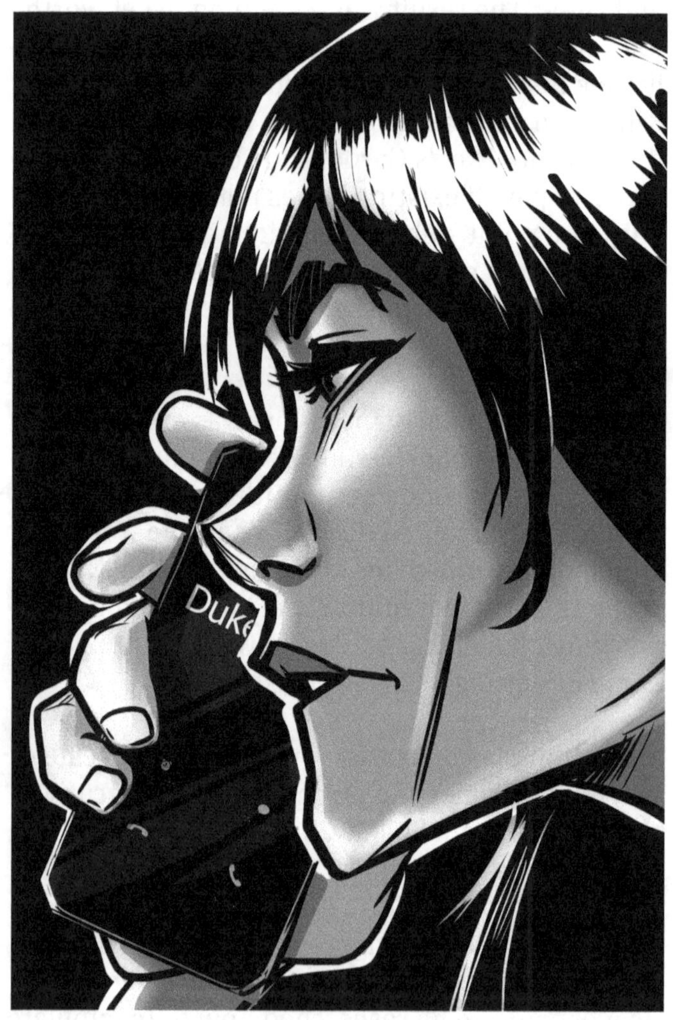


## THE PLAN

# 21
# The Plan

Shen's horse racing winnings allowed him to payoff his current casino debts and still have almost three million dollars to play with. This gave him leverage. He could demand playing concessions and if the King's Garden executives didn't agree, he could threaten to cash-in and move his business to a King's Garden competitor. All the casinos worked hard to poach big money whales from their competitors and Shen was an ideal potential candidate.

Shen decided to pay Pansy ten thousand dollars to accompany him to the baccarat table. She was to stand behind him for as long as he gambled whether that was for one hour or two days. All she had to do was bring him drinks when he needed one, otherwise, he told her, "Just be yourself," which meant continuously prattling on in Mandarin about anything she wanted.

Shen then went to Marcie demanding certain table changes or he would move his business to another casino. Marcie did not want to lose Shen's lucrative business, so she pressured the gaming executives to agree to Shen's demands: a specific brand of playing cards with an unusual diamond pattern on the back; an automatic card shuffler; use of the same eight decks of cards for as long as he was playing; and finally, a Chinese dealer that spoke Mandarin.

Shen only played high stakes baccarat in the private gambling rooms. Each baccarat table accommodated twelve players. The dealer, the pit boss, and security all had to keep their eyes on all the players looking for cheats. Whether Shen's scheme was actually cheating depends on which side of the table you're sitting on. What Shen was attempting to do was employ a particular form of advantage gambling known as edge sorting. Edge sorting isn't technically cheating although casino operators might argue to the contrary. All the concessions Shen demanded were an effort to allow him an opportunity to use edge sorting in order to move the odds on the baccarat table from a small built-in house advantage to a considerable five percent advantage in Shen's favour.

All playing cards have printed backs, most with complex geometric designs. During the manufacturing process the decks of cards are cut and trimmed to the standard regulation size, but like all production processes there is an acceptable tolerance that leads to slight irregularities in the visible edge patterns on the backs of the cards.

Normally this doesn't matter if decks of cards are constantly being removed from play and new ones added, or if the dealer hand shuffles the cards so that the edge of the card that appears in the shoe is constantly being changed. In order to eliminate this problem Shen demanded the use of the same eight decks of cards for as long as he played and the use of an automatic shuffler that guaranteed the same edge of each card would always appear in the shoe. Pansy's nonstop babbling was nothing more than a distraction, so that none of the official watchers would notice how much attention Shen was paying to the cards as they came out of the shoe. Shen's demand for a Mandarin speaking dealer wasn't just so Pansy would distract him but also because Chinese dealers have the reputation of working fast, and the faster a dealer worked, the more often the targeted cards would come out.

Punto Banco Baccarat is a very simple card game. It has been said the game was developed for some king who was too dumb to follow complicated rules; the tale is most likely false, but it does make for a good story and it illustrates the simplicity of a game designed to take your money as quickly as possible without much effort or skill. In any case, if Punto Banco was good enough for James Bond, it was good enough for Sammy Shen.

Players bet on either the Bank or the Player. It doesn't matter how many people are playing; they only have two choices, technically they do have a third, they could bet on a tie, but that is such a bad bet that it is rarely employed except maybe by novices on the mini baccarat table. The dealer slides four cards out of the shoe, two for the Player and two for the Bank. The dealer flips over the cards revealing the winner that is determined by whichever hand comes closest to nine with tens and picture cards counting as zero. Hands that total more than ten have ten deducted so a hand of five and six totals one. Hands of nine or eight automatically win. If a hand is five or less, a third card is dealt. That is all there is to the game. If an edge sorter can spot the irregularity on the back of a nine for example, he or she gains a tremendous advantage.

Shen plays for sixteen hours straight with Pansy babbling almost nonstop except for several brief pee breaks and occasional liquor runs to the bar. Shen turns his two point eight million dollars into seven million. The casino is not happy and accuses Shen of cheating. They refuse to pay and Shen threatens to sue. Shen's two point eight million bankroll is traced back to his racetrack winnings and a brief investigation determines that the trifecta bet was the result of a tip from one of the Cisco brothers who are accused of being in cahoots with Shen and Marcie Reynolds in order to cheat the casino.

Marcie and the brothers deny any involvement but nevertheless are blamed for the financial disaster. It's up to Marcie to cut a deal with Shen to minimize the casino's losses but Shen demands payment of the entire seven million dollars. Marcie has no choice but to call on the services of Duke Feng.

**DUKE FENG**

## 22
## Duke Feng

Duke Feng looked like your average young Hong Kong hipster with more money than taste. He wore stylish suits, custom shirts, and heavy gold jewellery. His hair was long and his outward manner charming, an asset in attracting young women to join his stable of high-priced escorts. But like many psychopaths, his easy manner and charming personality were only thin facades that barely masked Feng's true corroded personality. Duke Feng was a pimp and a thug, a combination of traits that made Feng useful to Marcie Reynolds.

Feng seemed to take an inordinate amount of pleasure out of applying the occasional beating to an over zealous john or obstinate debtor reluctant to pay what was owed. If one of Marcie's clients became a problem, one call to the Duke would usually resolve the issue. Feng used a series of escalating practices in order to collect the delinquent funds starting with intimidation and blackmail and ending in a call to the paramedics. When a debtor decides to be stubborn, it's amazing how much more effective a broken arm is than a severe scolding.

The situation with Shen was a little different. It was the casino that owed Shen the dough and not the other way around. When whales lose large sums of money, the casino will often cut a deal. Lose twenty-thousand-dollars and a thug like Feng shows up to break your leg; lose fifty million, and everybody wants to negotiate. The local Aussie King Garden's executives knew that a loss of seven million dollars would not go unnoticed. It would eventually meander its way through the complex series of numbered companies until it found its way onto the desks of Benson Yeung and Lee-Sam Park. That would not be good news for the Aussie suits. Yeung and Park are not men that you want to disturb with such matters. It was in everyone's interest that a settlement be reached, otherwise the family Cisco might end up at the bottom of the Barrier Reef with their namesake species, and the Aussie front men might not be far behind. Enter Duke Feng, chief MDP Excursion's negotiator.

Sammy Shen was a sophisticated Chinese bureaucrat; if he wasn't, he never would have risen to a position where he could lay his hands on enough loose cash to fund his increasing gambling addiction. When it came to politics Sammy knew when to push and when to keep a low profile. Running afoul of his political superiors meant certain exile to a re-education camp were good-old- Sammy would be taught the error of his ways; and if for some reason, he became obstinate, there was always prison or even in extreme cases of recalcitrance, the firing squad. So Sammy knew the score in the People's Republic, but the world of gambling was, and is, a different pot of rice. So for some mistaken reason, Sammy thought the West was different, and oh sure it is to an extent, but when you deal with organizations like the Hong Mian and the Pal-e Hyeongje, the consequences of pigheadedness can also be deadly, with the level of patience even shorter.

If Sammy didn't pay his debts to the casino, he understood he'd be in danger. Even if the casino didn't have him killed, a few choice words to the right government mandarin and Sammy would be marched blind-folded to the wall, and I don't mean the one Emperor Qin Shi Huang built. But now the flowerpot-sole shoe was on the other foot, and Sammy thought he had leverage. What he didn't understand was that the casino owing him seven million dollars was just as dangerous as him owing the casino.  Sammy was adamant, he wanted his dough; after all it was only right. He'd lost at least that much over the years and now it was time for payback.

Marcie tried to reason with Sammy and explained that she was authorized to offer him a one point two million cash payment plus a considerable number of complimentary casino services, but Sammy wouldn't consider it. Marcie warned him of the dangers of his stubborn attitude, and the consequences of his intransigence. He demanded to see Marcie's bosses. Her bosses were not pleased, with Sammy or with Marcie for that matter, but being big shots, they thought they could handle this overreaching asshole with a combination of carrot and stick. A meeting was set up for Saturday at 10:00 PM at the Law Offices of Richard Tyler. Rich Tyler was one of the casino's lawyers, the one who handled cases like Sammy Shen.

When Shen arrived at the offices of Richard Tyler he was greeted in the lobby by Marcie Reynolds. No one else was there, after all it was Saturday evening and all the lawyers, secretaries, and subordinate staff were enjoying their weekend. Marcie greets Shen warmly with assurances that everything will be resolved this evening. Marcie takes Shen into a large elegant boardroom decorated in a manner befitting a law firm that handled clients like the King's Garden Casino. Present in the boardroom were Richard Tyler and to Shen's surprise Duke Feng. Shen looks at Feng and then at Tyler.

Shen: "Why is he here?"

Tyler: "It's Ms. Reynold's company MDP Excursions that is responsible for bringing you to the King's Garden and is ultimately responsible for you whether you win or lose at the tables. Mr. Feng is a subcontractor for MDP and as such has a significant stake in what you decide this evening. So you see Sammy... I can call you Sammy can't I?" Sammy nods. "That's great," says Tyler, "we're all friends here, right?" Sammy reluctantly nods again.

Shen: "Look... I want my money, all of it! I won it fair and square. I've always paid my debts to you and I expect you to do the same." Marcie and Feng sit quietly not saying a word.

Tyler: "Well our position... Sammy... is, you cheated, and we don't owe you anything..."

Feng: "Except maybe..." Tyler shoots Feng a lawyer's look, and Feng's words tail off to a murmured, "...settlement." Not exactly the sentiment he was about to express.

Shen: "No dice! I didn't cheat and I want my money!"

Tyler opens a brown legal-sized leather folder. He pulls out what looks like a legal document, along with a cheque paper-clipped to the corner. Tyler unclips the cheque from the document and pushes both across the boardroom table towards Shen. He reaches into his Brioni Vanquish suit jacket pocket and takes out a Mont Blanc, Limited Edition, Miles Davis Fountain Pen. He places it on top of the document. Tyler points a long elegant manicured finger, flashing a two-carat diamond set in black onyx, at the document. "This my friend Sammy, is a release acknowledging that your baccarat winnings were the result of an edge sorting scheme that you knowingly and with intent, perpetrated on King's Garden Entertainment LLC by asking for concessions under the guise of catering to your superstitions rather than the truth which is these concessions were demanded so that you could edge sort, which is expressly forbidden by the casino."

Shen: " Now wait just a minute..."

Tyler ignores Shen's objections and continues, "Further more, you acknowledge that you hired Pansy Ping, an escort, and paid her ten thousand dollars to distract the baccarat dealer while you cheated."

Shen shouts, "I DID NOT CHEAT!"

Tyler doesn't pay any attention to Shen's outburst, "However..." Tyler points his diamond encrusted finger at the cheque, tapping it several times, "we acknowledge that you are a valued customer and since English is not your native language, it is possible that you did not read, or that you read, but did not understand the King's Garden Casino rules for playing baccarat. And as such, we are offering you seven hundred and twenty-five thousand dollars in good faith as a gesture of our appreciation as a valued client." Shen starts screaming obvious curses in Mandarin.

Tyler: "English please Sammy, my Chinese is not that good, and I don't understand how my mother figures into this conversation."

Shen: "Seven hundred thousand... you already offered me one point two..."

Tyler: "I'm sad to say that was then, and this is now. When you refused Ms. Reynolds generous offer, the casino turned the case over to me, and various circumstances came to light."

Shen: "What are you talking about? What circumstances?"

Tyler: "... the intentional misleading of the casino in regard to why you wanted various concessions at the baccarat table; your intention to use edge sorting, expressly forbidden by the casino; and your hiring of Pansy Ping in order to mislead, confuse, and distract the dealer from properly performing his official duties. The fact is Sammy, seven hundred..."

Shen interrupts, "You bastards..." He pauses to catch his breath. "All right, I'll take the one point two million and sign your release." He pushes the release and the cheque back towards Tyler.

Tyler: "I'm afraid one point two is off the table. And if we leave this room without a signed release, the current seven hundred and twenty-five thousand offer, will also be off the table. The decision is yours Sammy, you can accept the current offer, or get nothing."

Shen reaches out and picks up the cheque to look at it. "It's not even certified."

Tyler: "I assure you Sammy, the cheque is good."

Shen stands. He grabs Tyler's pen. He notices its unique design and figures it must be worth a lot of money. He signs the release. "And I'm keeping the fucking pen." He grabs the cheque, stuffs it in his suit jacket. "Bastards! All of you are bastards!" His taunt comes out almost apologetically. He's defeated. He leaves.

Marcie turns to Feng, "You know what to do." Feng gets up and leaves.

Tyler: "I didn't hear that."

Marcie: "Hear what? I didn't say anything."

The next morning the maids at the Sky Harbour Hotel had trouble opening the door to Room 2037. When security was finally able to push the door open, they found Pansy Ping and Sammy Shen dead on the floor in front of the door. Pansy had her throat cut and Sammy had a hole in what was left of his head. The police ruled the incident a murder-suicide between two lovers. No cheque was ever found or cashed. The next morning Pauley Cisco leaves for California and Marcie Reynolds is transferred to another KG casino in Macau.

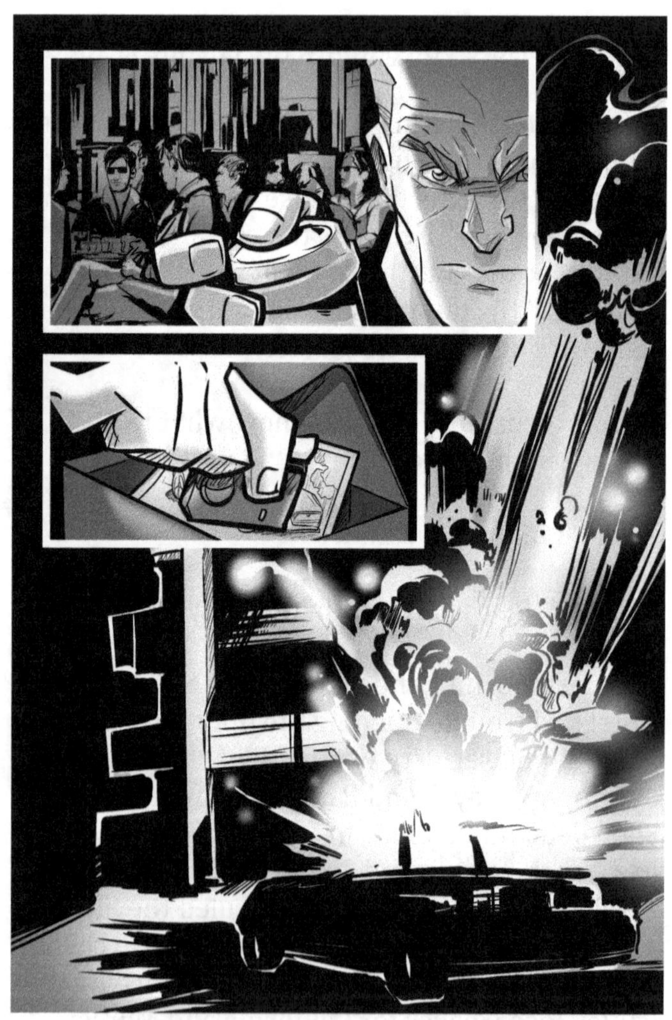

**A JOB SUITED FOR THE TAILOR**

## 23
## A Job Suited For The Tailor

Hong Kong's vibrant nightlife is concentrated in the Tsim Sha Tsui, Lan Kwai Fong, and Wan Chai districts. Tonight, Duke Feng is hosting a stag party for one of his clients at the Laughing Monkey Club, once owned by the late Charlie Long, the deposed Dragon Head of the now defunct Wan Chai triad. The current absentee owner of the club is William Stone. Feng has taken over the biggest private party room in the club and has populated it with his entire entourage of exotic executives.

The party features drinking, music, dancing, karaoke, and sex, as its main attractions. Around four in the morning the party starts to break up. A few incapacitated stragglers are left in various states of inebriation waiting to gain the courage to take on the coming morning light. Duke Feng is pleased with the night's receipts and the potential new clients that can be lured to the King's Garden. Marcie Reynolds may be gone, but he has confidence he is still a valuable asset supplying well-heeled marks to fill the baccarat seats in the private gaming rooms of the King Garden's Casino.

Unfortunately for Feng, his self-appraisal is an acute overestimation of his value to the corporation. Men like Duke Feng are a Hong Kong dollar-a-dozen. His involvement in the tragic and un-timely murder-suicide of Pansy Ping and Sammy Shen make him a loose end, a nasty irritable thread that could possibly unravel the whole damn operation. Loose ends need to be cut-off, tied-up, and eliminated.

Duke leaves the Laughing Monkey. The steamy morning air hits his face like a dash of reality. He hands his parking ticket to the waiting car jockey, who disappears into the early morning light straining to gain a foothold on the day. Across the street sitting at a table in an outdoor café is a well-dressed man nursing a cappuccino. Mo Fields has been patiently waiting for his target to appear. The car jockey is Hong Mian. That morn-ing he received a package sent to his apartment. Inside the package were a black box and a pic-ture of Duke Feng and his Jaguar F-Type Sports car.  Also in the package was a set of instructions on where to place the device on the undercar-riage of the Jag. The device was a small black box about the size of a packet of cigarettes. It was a simple gadget with only one button and two lights, one red and one green. The red light was on.  There was also a package of matches. Once the button was pressed the red light would turn green and the device would be armed. After the gizmo was placed under the Jag, the car jockey was to burn the instructions and the package it came in.

Mo Fields' eyes never leave the front of the Laughing Monkey. Feng finally comes out and hands the car jockey his ticket. The car jockey disappears into the parking garage around the corner. In a few minutes the bright cherry red Jaguar F-Type screeches to a halt in front of the Laughing Monkey. Feng hands the jockey a twenty-dollar note and gets into his car. He puts the car in gear and heads down the almost vacant street. Fields waits till the Jag clears several drunken tourists making their way back to their hotel. He takes out his phone and dials a number. The cherry red Jaguar F-Type and Duke Feng explode in a ball of fire. Car parts mixed with body parts are hurled fifty yards in all directions, taking out a few shop windows as they find their smouldering resting places. Fields leaves a substantial tip for the café owner who stayed open late to accommodate the rich American. Fields finishes his cappuccino, placing the cup and saucer in a paper bag he kept in his pocket especially for this purpose. Fields gets up and heads back to his room at the Peninsula Hotel. It's close to the dock, the perfect place to dump the cup and saucer. Never leave evidence; it was standard tradecraft.

**AND FINALLY**

# 24
# Epilogue

**And Finally...**
The meeting at the SIB Bank didn't take long. Once Jesse and Stone arrived things started to move quickly. Pauley looks at Jesse and Stone, and then at the Female Bank Executive, "Why are they here? Is the Englishman here to kill us?"

Park: "Don't be silly. Mr. Stone is here to represent the interests of Benson Yeung and Johnny Luck."

Pauley waves in the direction of Jesse, "So what about her?"

Park: "Ms. James and Mr. Stone are kind of an entry. You're familiar with the racing term I'm sure."

This kind of talk makes Mr. Shinn, the bank President, and his executive very nervous. They don't like the turn the conversation has taken. The Female Bank Executive notices her boss's discomfort, "Mr. Cisco, you are sitting in the boardroom of the Seoul International Bank; South Korea's most prestigious banking institution. We don't kill people; we just take their money."

At this point, Mr. Shinn stands. The Female Executive, Jesse, Stone, and Park, all stand as well. Pauley and Marcie figure they should also stand.

Shinn bows to Jesse, Stone, and Park, acknowledging his subordinate with a somewhat perfunctory nod. He leaves ignoring Pauley and Marcie completely. Everyone sits leaving Pauley and Marcie standing.

Jesse looks at the two of them still standing, bewildered, "Sit the fuck down, we're not finished with you two yet." Pauley and Marcie sit. "You want to know why we're here; it's really very simple. You fuck with my racetrack; there are consequences; you fuck with the Hong Mian, and the consequences can be deadly." Jesse turns to Stone. She reaches out to touch his hand and says in a tone that is almost a purr, "He's here because he's the one I fuck the most."

The Female Bank Executive, blushes, stifles a giggle, and speaks, "Mr. Stone is a financial advisor who's here to look after your substantial bank deposit. The funds your partner unfairly appropriated from Mr. Park. We acknowledge that it was not you or Miss Reynolds that scammed SKE-Sport, but you did force Mr. Park to go to extraordinary measures and considerable expensive including the unfortunate and untimely demise of Mr. Kim in order to find out what actually occurred. In that regard, Mr. Park is demanding compensation."

Pauley: "What kind of compensation are we talking about?"

The Female Bank Executive: "I'll let Mr. Park explain."

Park: "As a senior executive at a major Macau casino, you Miss Reynolds, have value. As a trainer of thoroughbred racehorses, Mr. Cisco, you too, might be useful. In other words, we're asking, demanding really, that you do our two organizations an occasional favour. Agreed?"

Pauley: "Okay fine, we'd be happy to do that." He turns to Marcie, "Right dear?" Marcie nods.

Park: "I need you to say it out loud."

Marcie almost stuttering, "Yes, of course, I'll do whatever you ask."

Pauley: "And what about the money? I assume you're going to take that too?"

Stone: "I believe that's where I come in."

The Female Bank Executive takes a series of legal documents out of her leather folio. She stands and takes them to the other end of the table where Pauley and Marcie are sitting. She places one set of documents in front of Marcie and another in front of Pauley. "Miss Reynolds, please sign where indicated by the green sticky tab and Mr. Cisco, you please sign anywhere there is a yellow sticky tab."

Marcie looks at Stone. "What are we signing?"

Stone: "Does it matter?" Marcie and Pauley both shake their heads. The Female Bank Executive turns the pages of both sets of documents pointing to various places marked with green and yellow sticky tabs.

Stone continues, "I suppose there's no reason not to tell you what you're signing. One document is a Power of Attorney, allowing me complete access to your funds and control over how those funds are managed. The other two documents are Wills, one for each of you, leaving your estates to a numbered company in the Isle of Man." Pauley and Marcie complete signing the documents.

Pauley looks at Stone and then at Park, "If we're done, we'd like to leave."

Park answers, "Of course... you are free to go and enjoy your new lives in Macau. In fact we have arranged for a limo to take you directly to the airport. There are two first class tickets waiting for you at the Air Macau counter."

Pauley: "That won't be necessary, we need to go back to the hotel and checkout. We can find our own way from there."

Jesse: "Don't be silly. We insist, and besides it would be an insult to Mr. Park if you don't accept his offer." Mo Fields enters the boardroom wearing a nicely tailored chauffeur's uniform. Jesse gives Pauley a very hard look. "We really do insist."

Mo leads Pauley Cisco and Marcie Reynolds out of the boardroom and down to his waiting limo parked directly in front of the bank. Mo opens the back door and signals Pauley and Marcie to get in. He closes the limo door. Mo gets in the front seat. The glass partition that divides the front driver's seat from the back passenger seats is already raised. The noises from the street are completely deadened. The sound of the door locks is almost deafening. Pauley taps on the glass partition. Mo ignores it. He pulls into traffic heading for the highway.

Pauley Cisco and Marcie Reynolds never make it to Macau. There were rumours about a botched kidnapping, but nobody ever received a ransom note and no bodies were ever recovered. To this day nobody knows what happened to Pauley Cisco and Marcie Reynolds.

**THE END**

**THE OUTLAW RIDER**

**DEAD END**

**PALERMO**

**STONE COLD**